ELEVENTH
GRADE STRESS

BRUCE INGRAM

SECANT
PUBLISHING

For information about this title, contact the publisher:

Secant Publishing, LLC
P.O. Box 79
Salisbury, MD 21803

www.secantpublishing.com

ISBN 978-1-944962-61-6 (paperback)
Library of Congress Control Number: 2019937284

Printed in the United States of America

I am grateful to the following teachers and staff
at Lord Botetourt High School and elsewhere
in the public school system who contributed
invaluable perspectives and insights:

Melissa Amos
Carrie Baldacci
Megan Biggio
Rob Campbell
Amanda Collins
Jessica Curulla
Doak Harbison
Christine Haxton
Whitney Hughes
Mary Lewis
Kendel Lively
Michael Martin
Christen Myers
Don Rice
Shelly Roberts

The following students in my Creative Writing II-IV
classes helped edit the book for grammar and content:

McKayla Hoke
Taylor Jones
Jessica Lancenese
Abby Martin
Anna Rosenberger
Shanelle Smith

The following students in my Creative Writing II-IV classes edited the final copy for grammar and content:

Alyssa Brader
Maia Folk
Karsen Hazlelwood
Baylee Howell
Hailee Link
Elizabeth Spencer

These Creative Writing students read the final copy for content:

Allison Combe
Madison Gunther
Nikki Imamander
Zander Lenoir
Madison Mullins
Angel Swain

Also, special thanks to educators Peter Lewis and Karen Carroll for their help.

BACK TO SCHOOL

CHAPTER ONE

LUKE

I still miss Mia. I miss kissing her, holding her hand, talking to her on the phone before I go to bed… just doing anything with her. When she called right after school ended to tell me that she couldn't see me anymore, it broke my heart. I know that her parents were fighting all the time over our relationship. Her mom was accepting of me, but her dad couldn't stand me. And I understood—and respected her decision—when she said that we couldn't be the reason that her parents might break up. And I understand why Mia didn't feel that we could continue to date secretly, like we had our entire sophomore year. Sooner or later, her dad would find out, just like he did last May.

The last time we talked over the phone, Mia said that we should promise each other that when our ten-year high school reunion came around, if both of us were still single, we would get married. She'd almost be finished with medical school and out on her own. I promised her; but the more I thought about it over the summer, the more I realized we're never going to be together again. I know she meant what she said; but she's too smart, she's too pretty, she's too perfect in every way not to meet some fantastic guy somewhere along the way and fall in love with him.

So I've got to try to put her out of mind, hopefully find

someone new, try to get my grades up, get ready for college... get on with my life. One of the best gifts Mia gave me was the gift of self-confidence. I am somebody; and I'm not a loser, which my dad kept hammering into me. I can have a wonderful life. I can get through anything. Both my parents died last year, and I survived that. I've got to keep believing that I am somebody when school starts to suck, or some jerk bullies me, or a girl won't go out with me because she thinks I'm some kind of lower-class loser.

I guess my first "test" was when I dropped by school a few days before classes started so I could pick up my schedule. My guidance counselor, Mrs. Whitney, told me that I needed to go see Mrs. Elliott. I knew that couldn't be good because she's head of the special ed department. I saw that Algebra II wasn't on my schedule, but something called Algebra Functions and Data Analysis was. Sounds like an "Algebra for People Too Stupid to Take Algebra II" class, if you ask me.

Sure enough, it was; but that wasn't the worst of it. Mrs. Elliott said my past math grades "were a concern," and that she and Mrs. Whitney had decided to do a "Child Study" on me and see if I might qualify for "Special Education Services." Look, I know I've got problems in math. I've made a *D* or *F* every grading period since eighth grade, but I'm 16; why do they have to call it a "Child Study?" It's humiliating enough to be labeled a special-ed student, but to be called a *child* just makes the whole thing worse.

I'll say one thing for Mrs. Elliott: she couldn't have been nicer when she was talking to me. She said the Algebra Functions class was just a way of "providing you with some additional support before you go into Algebra II in your senior year." Well, what if I fail Algebra Functions? The only reason I passed Algebra I and Geometry was because Mia was tutoring me. And those remedial classes can be a zoo—filled with stupid-in-math people like me who don't know what's going on and hate being there.

Then Mrs. Elliott started talking about the Child Study. "We just want to see if you might be eligible for some *accommodations* in the classroom, or *possibly* be eligible for Special Education Services."

I teared up when she said that. I tried to hide it from her, but I couldn't. "Luke," she said, "nobody is going to single you out as being stupid if you're found to qualify for Special Education Services. We want to provide you with support to make you successful."

"Provide support because I'm stupid!" I blurted out. And doesn't she realize that there are too many students in this school who bully the slower kids—and make remarks about them in the cafeteria and in the halls?

"No, you're not stupid," she said. "We need to work on your weaknesses, and you shouldn't be ashamed of that. The school can even send your Special Education paperwork, if you are classified that way, to college so that you can receive extra services there."

Oh, great. So now some college that I want to go to, if they even let me in at all, is going to know I'm too dumb to pass regular math. With all those really smart kids trying to get into a college and there not being room for all of them, how am I supposed to get in with "special services needed" next to my name? What college is going to want somebody like me to "ma-tric-u-late" in their institute of higher learning?

Mrs. Elliott could see that I was upset and kept reassuring me, and she was really nice about it. I left her and went to see Mr. Guthridge, the cross country coach. I told him that I had been running a lot all summer, and was ready to start the season. Then I went home, mowed two neighborhood lawns, and ran five miles. I'm glad I'm almost through with my lawn-mowing business; there won't be any time for that with all these hard classes I'm taking this year, plus running cross country.

CHAPTER TWO

ELLY

I've never felt so unhappy in my entire life. I always thought that if I lost weight, got contacts, let my hair grow long, and found a hot guy to be my boyfriend, my life would be awesome. After all, my family lives in an upper-class neighborhood. And I might as well admit it: my mom and dad have pampered and spoiled me my whole life—me, the oldest child and only girl. They've forgiven me every time I've messed up and lied to them, and I still don't seem to have learned anything from all my screw-ups. And the consequences that Mom and Dad keep promising would happen rarely do, and the punishments they hand out don't ever last as long as they say they will.

My good-looking boyfriend is the main reason I'm so miserable. When Caleb and I started dating last May, I was so thrilled. I had tried to flirt with him and get him to notice me for ages, but he never did until I made those changes in my appearance. Maybe that should have been the first warning sign about him. If I hadn't lost those 20-plus pounds last year, there's no way he would have ever asked me out. From the very beginning of our relationship, he has tried to control everything I do. I had to leave such and such weekend open for him. I couldn't even talk to other boys. I couldn't go to a photography workshop over the summer because it "conflicted" with something he wanted us to go do.

The weekend his family and mine spent at the beach together right before school started was absolutely the worst. On our last night there, we told our parents that we were going to an amusement park, but we went driving around instead. Later, he started drinking some kind of rum that he had brought from his parents' liquor cabinet. After what happened last year with my ex (Matthew and I were in a wreck because he and I were both drunk), I didn't want to do any more drinking-and-driving type of stuff. So I told him that I didn't want any rum, and he shouldn't drink and drive; and that maybe I should drive us back to the rental house.

He got so furious that he pulled the car over. "You'll do what I tell you to do," he yelled at me. "Don't you ever tell me what to do or how to drive!" He then grabbed my left wrist and twisted it and started squeezing. It hurt so bad that I started crying and begged him to stop.

He then said, "I'm going to ask you again. Do you want any rum? What's your answer gonna be?"

"Yes," I said, and he made me drink two plastic cups of rum and coke on the way back to the rental.

I don't see how he wasn't pulled over on the way back. He was swerving all over the road. We were lucky not to have wrecked. When we got back, he told me that we were going down to the beach behind the rental… that it would be "private back there." I got really scared when he said that. I was so dizzy and sick from the rum and his terrible driving that I felt like throwing up.

When we were walking down behind the house, he started throwing up; and I decided that was my chance to get away from him. I left him on the beach, puking. The next morning, Mom asked me about my bruised wrist. I told her that I had injured it on one of the amusement park rides. What's one more lie after all the others I've told her? When our families went out to eat breakfast before going back home, Caleb acted like nothing had happened. He didn't seem to notice that Mom had put an ACE bandage on my wrist.

When we got back home, I told Mom that I had been thinking about breaking up with Caleb. She told me that whatever he had done, I should give him "one more chance." After all, she said, she and dad were "such good friends with his family." And dad and Caleb's father have all these "business dealings" and we all "go to the same church."

I should have told her about what happened on our last night there. What on earth is the matter with me that I can't seem to do the smart thing? I don't need an abusive boyfriend. I've got enough stress on me with school starting and all these hard classes on my schedule. I've got A.P. English first period, then A.P. U.S. History, Advanced Chemistry, Algebra II, Spanish III, Art I, and Yearbook II last. Art will be fun; and Yearbook will give me a chance to keep working on my photography skills, which will be fantastic. But those first five classes will mean a lot of notes and test-taking. A.P. English and History will mean tons of reading and research papers. I just don't see how I can handle all of these assignments.

Mom also said that I need to think about which college I'm going to go to. I've got to complete all these applications, and we need to make some college visits this fall. And wouldn't it be great, Mom said, if Caleb and I ended up at the same college? "Maybe he will want to go on some of our visits," she said.

I dread being around him. Yet, I'm supposed to meet him after the football game on Friday night for pizza, and we're going to a movie on Saturday night. I hate myself.

CHAPTER THREE

MARCUS

Last Friday, we played the first game of the football season. I finally got to play again; but we lost, and I played terribly. I argued with Mom and Dad all summer that I was ready to play, and that I was fully recovered from my concussion and leg injuries. Finally, Dad gave in first when I was talking to him in private, and he promised he would convince Mom. But even after she did come around to our point of view, she wasn't happy about me playing.

Matthew and I were the starting receivers; and before the game started, Caleb told me he was planning on keeping us "real busy." Jefferson, the team we were playing, won only four times last season and lost its best players to graduation. Plus, it was a home game for us, and the stands were packed. So, we were heavy favorites to win. On our first possession on third and five, Coach Dell called for me to run a slant over the middle, and Caleb's pass was right on target... I dropped it.

I almost always get hit by a linebacker or a safety—and sometimes both—when I run a slant across the middle. All I could think of when I was running the pattern was that somebody was going to hit me. My mind was on that instead of the ball. Sure enough, a couple of Jefferson guys slammed me anyway when the ball slipped through my fingers.

When our offensive team got back to the bench, Caleb

started cussing me out to get my head in the game. I lost my temper and got up in his face, and Matthew and Tito had to separate us. Then Coach Dell came over and yelled at all of us. Things just got worse after that.

Jefferson marched down the field on this long, time-consuming drive that ate up much of the first quarter. They kept the ball on the ground almost the entire time, getting four or five yards on almost every run—finally scoring a touchdown on a quarterback sneak.

When we got the ball back with about three minutes left in the quarter, Jefferson stuffed our first two running plays. Then Coach Dell called for a long pass to me, and Caleb underthrew the ball. The cornerback covering me intercepted it and ran it all the way back for a Pick 6. We got back to the bench; and, again, Caleb started yelling at me, sprinkling in a few of his favorite four-letter words. He told me that when I saw that the ball was underthrown, I should have come back for it. That's just bull. I didn't make him throw a wild pass.

Nobody scored again for the rest of the game. Jefferson kept the ball on the ground all night. They'd make it to about midfield, punt, and pin us way back near the goal line. Caleb would throw a few bad passes or we'd only make a few yards running the ball, then Caleb would sail the ball over Matthew's head or mine. I just couldn't seem to get separation from the Jefferson cornerback.

On Monday's practice after the first day of school, Coach Dell told me and Caleb to stay after practice because he wanted to talk to us individually in his office. I figured he was going to discipline us for what had happened last Friday night, but it was much worse than that. In fact, he didn't even mention our arguing on the sidelines.

Coach talked to Caleb first, and it wasn't long before I heard Caleb raise his voice and blame Matthew and me for his bad throws. Next, I heard Dell raise his voice; and he said, "Don't you ever show disrespect for me again. Do it again, boy, and you'll be watching this Friday's game from the bleachers."

Things got real quiet after that. A few minutes later, Caleb came out of Dell's office and blurted out, "Because of you, I've lost the starting quarterback job." I started to say something back, but Caleb was at least partly right. I haven't played well in practice or in the first game. When we did our 40-yard sprints back in July, I found that I've lost two-tenths of a second since my freshman year. Because of my leg injury, I'm not getting faster. I'm slower than I was when I was a freshman.

So, I wasn't really surprised when Coach Dell told me that I had lost my starting job to Tito; and that now, I was going to be the third and long receiver. He also asked me if I wanted to maybe play some on defense, be the nickelback on sure passing downs and perhaps even play on special teams some. It was so depressing, but he was right. I'm not getting the job done. I told him that, and I promised to work hard in practice.

"Marcus, I really appreciate your positive attitude," he said. "I know you've gone through a lot with two major injuries in the past year. I'd like for you to work with Tito and show him a few things. He and Antonio are both pretty green, but they have a lot of potential." So, Antonio's the new quarterback; and he and Tito—two freshmen—have replaced me and Caleb. How ironic... we sent two upperclassmen to the bench when we joined varsity in ninth grade, and now that's happened to us.

When I got home, the first thing I did was go to my room and call Joshua at college. I told him all about what had happened after practice, and he told me that he was proud of me for taking my demotion like a man. I needed my brother to say something nice to me. He told me to keep working hard in practice and school, and things would work out alright.

I appreciated him saying that, but "things" aren't going to work out alright. Those dreams I had of playing pro football back when I was a freshman now seem immature and ridiculous. I'm never going to play pro football. I probably never had a chance anyway, leg injury or not. I'm not going to even be able to play football at a D-1 school in college. It's time I concentrated on just school and basketball.

CHAPTER FOUR

MIA

I spent the summer being angry—no, sullen is the right word… "showing irritation through a gloomy silence"—at my parents, especially my poppa. Mama, at least, initially took my side when Poppa told me that I had to break up with Luke. But even she eventually gave in to my father (that's what I call him now to his face; I'm not going to honor him by calling him Poppa) because she said she was worn out from fighting him 24/7.

How can my parents demand that I be responsible enough to become valedictorian of my class, work as a babysitter on weekend nights, have dinner on the table when they get home from work, start my two sisters on their homework when we get home from school, and take care of the chickens and the yard? Yet not be mature and responsible enough, to make a decision on what boy I want to be with? Luke treated me like a queen, treated me with respect and tenderness, the whole time we were together in our freshman and sophomore years. What more could any girl want? Yet to my father, he wasn't good enough because Luke is poor and white. Well, we're poor and Hispanic. How many people in this country look down on people like us, and question whether we even belong here?

I am so stressed out over the Luke thing, and the work

my parents keep piling on me. Plus, today was the first day of school, and I've never had a schedule this hard. Last spring, my guidance counselor, Mrs. Whitney, told me that since I want to be a doctor, I need to get a jump on college by taking some college-level classes at the local community college. She arranged for me to take Human Anatomy and Physiology I, Medical Terminology, and Introduction to Philosophy in the mornings at the college; then come to school and take A.P. English 11, A.P. U.S. History, Advanced Chemistry, and Calculus. That's seven college-level or advanced classes every day with hours and hours of homework every night. There were no openings for me to take Yearbook II (where I could have at least been in the same class as Luke for the only time all day) or any other electives. My father told me before school started that I was not to take any classes with Luke, and to have no contact with him whatsoever. Oh, and by the way, have his dinner hot for him when he gets home.

Well, I'm not going to have his dinner *hot* for him anymore. There's simply no time. Besides, I'm tired of being his servant. When I got home from school today, I was overrun with homework and reading assignments. I had at least six hours of work to do between college and high school, and it was just the first day. Before my parents got home, all I had time to finish was the Human Anatomy assignment on current trends in cell and tissue research.

My father came into my room and wanted to know where dinner was. I tried to explain to him that I had six-plus hours of homework to do; and if I were lucky, I'd be done by 11:00 P.M. Maybe I shouldn't have said what I said next, but I was so furious at him that I got sarcastic. "If you can wait until 11:30, I can cook you a hot dinner. Or you can wait until I clean out the chicken run and gather eggs, and we'll have dinner at midnight. Or would you rather eat an early breakfast? Your choice. I'm your happy, smiling servant, just waiting to be ordered around."

He erupted in rage and screamed at me. For the first time

in my life, I screamed back at him. Mama then came into the room and took my side. She said that Poppa had to understand the stress that I would be under this year, that she would fix dinner tonight and every night, and that Poppa would just have to get used to eating a little later. Then they went off into the kitchen, still arguing.

I didn't come out of my room until around 7:30, when I had finished my Medical Terminology and Philosophy homework assignments. I just wanted to make myself a quick sandwich and get back to work. Mama and my father were on opposite sides of the living room; and obviously, they weren't doing any talking. Mama sweetly offered to heat up some leftovers for me, but I told her no and that I knew she was tired, too. I didn't make eye contact with my father. I didn't even want to acknowledge his presence.

Last week, he told me that he had been talking to the father of one of the college boys, Miguel, who goes to our Catholic church. My father said he learned that Miguel is not dating anyone, and that the "young man knows who you are and would be interested in dating you." Well, well, well, isn't that wonderful. My father has got somebody all picked out for me. I'm just a poor, dumb, little Mexican girl with no sense. Maybe he's even managed to have run a blood test on the young man to make sure he's a 100-percent Catholic Hispanic.

Maybe I should have said yes when Luke asked me to date him secretly this year. I miss him so much. Maybe I will try to get back together with him later in the year if Poppa settles down some. But if Poppa catches us a second time…

First Week of School

CHAPTER FIVE

LUKE

I was really looking forward to first-period English 11 A.P. with Ms. Roche because English is my favorite subject, and I'd heard that she's a good teacher. When I got to class, I sat down next to Allen and Paige—they've been dating since freshman year, which is pretty rare. Paige said she wanted to talk to me after class, and all I could think of was "What on earth for?" Then I saw Elly and Caleb come in and sit down together; and she said something, and he told her to shut up loud enough that everyone heard it.

I hate that kind of macho crap that people like Caleb are all about. That's no way to talk to a girl, especially somebody like Elly who is so perfect in so many ways. I've always liked Elly a lot. Back in ninth grade, I sometimes thought about getting the courage one day to ask her out... that is, before Mia came along. But now that Mia and I will never be together again, maybe I will ask Elly out. I don't care if she is going out with Caleb. So what if she turns me down? At least, I would have tried. And if she were to say yes...

Ms. Roche started the year off with a writing prompt. "You all need to take the prompt as practice for the state test. But more importantly, you need it so I can judge your writing abilities and adjust my lessons to meet those abilities."

The prompt was on whether we think the minimum

driving age should be raised. Everybody in the room probably already has their driver's license; of course, nobody wants the minimum driving age raised... duh. What a stupid, juvenile prompt; what a boring waste of time. But what really ticked me off was the emphasis on the state test in English. I understand the need to write better; that's important. But we're going to be spending a lot of time, Ms. Roche said, on preparing for the reading section of the state test. Translated from teacher-speak, that means we're going to learn how to make lucky guesses and bubble in line after line of multiple-guess questions.

Next, she gave us a bunch of literary terms, the same ones we get every year "because they are going to be on the state test." I know the difference between a simile and metaphor. I know what personification is. Ms. Roche next gave us the class syllabus, and then I got excited about reading some neat stuff. I was hoping to see books like *Walden* and *Adventures of Huckleberry Finn* because last year, the librarian, Mrs. Kendel, told Mia and me that they were some of the best books ever. Mrs. Kendel said they were standard eleventh-grade works. *Walden*, she said, is about this guy who goes off in the woods and lives by himself and thinks about life—how awesome is that? Mia and I ended up reading it in our two-person book club, and it would just have been great to read it again and discuss it in class. And Mrs. Kendel said that Huck Finn was a "coming-of-age odyssey." That's probably the best thing ever written in American literature.

I was so mad about the prompt and the literary terms and no *Walden* or *Huck Finn* on the reading list that I lost my temper, raised my hand, and started complaining about the syllabus. I didn't want to get off on the wrong foot with Ms. Roche, but this was just crap.

"We can't read *Huck Finn* because of the N-word and the racial slurs," she said. "The book might be offensive to some people."

All of a sudden, Marcus' hand shot up; and I could tell

that he was ticked, too. "I'm offended because you think I'd be offended," he said. "I know people were using the N-word in the 1800s—they still use it now in this school. I don't see why we can't read it."

"Censorship is wrong," added Kylee, Marcus' girlfriend. "*Huck Finn* is a classic. We need to read it for college."

People all over the room were arguing about whether to read it or not. Finally, Ms. Roche said, "We can read *Huck Finn* if everybody brings a note from home stating that you have permission to do so."

That settled everybody down until we started reading the first novel of the year, *The Scarlet Letter*. I've never read anything so mind-bogglingly boring in my whole life—long paragraphs written in like Old English, no dialog between the characters, and a plot that's going nowhere fast.

Finally, class ended; and Paige told me what she had wanted to say. "I've got this friend who's interested in you," she said. "Would you like to double-date on Saturday night with me and Allen?"

My mind started racing on who the girl might be. I know that Paige's best friends are Elly and Mia, so it's a pretty safe bet that it's neither one of them. I need to move on from Mia and start getting to know other girls, so I said yes. On Saturday night, I found out just who the girl was when they came to pick me up at Granddaddy's and my house—Mary, the class gossip. I can't stand her. She's pretty and in a lot of my classes, but she's an airhead and chases after guys all the time. I don't think most guys—at least the ones with any sense—want a girl like that. It's like she's desperate for a guy all the time, and is constantly breaking up or being dumped by her boyfriend of the week.

We got to the mall where the movie theater was. Mary flirted, smiled, and laughed at whatever I said. She touched me on my arms and back, and grabbed my hand and held it while we were walking around before the movie. Oh god, I couldn't stand being around her. Her conversation was all about stupid stuff: why we lost the football game on Friday night, did I know that so-and-so broke up the other day, that she had bought a new skirt... meh.

All night, I kept thinking about Mia and all the great times we had together; and here I was, wandering around a shopping mall with this suck-up airhead. During the movie, Mary leaned over and kissed me on the cheek and squeezed my hand, and all I could think about was how desperate she always acts around guys.

About half an hour after they dropped me off, Allen called to apologize. "No problem, man, it wasn't your fault," I said.

"Paige told me to tell you that she was sorry for the whole thing, too," Allen said. "She said Mary had been nagging her for about two weeks to set up a date with you."

Well, I know two things: that's my first and last date with Mary, and I'm not ever going to let some girl set me up with one of her friends again.

CHAPTER SIX

ELLY

The first week of school was awful, and the weekend was even worse. On the first day of school, Caleb started criticizing me as soon as he picked me up. He asked me if I had gained weight recently, and I said no; then he told me I probably needed to lose five pounds—that my legs were chubby. To make him happy, I had worn one of my shortest mini-skirts and a low-cut blouse that he has complimented me about before. I told him that I was trying to make him happy; and he said, "Well, you're not trying real hard. Ditch those five pounds."

In first-period A.P. English, he told me to shut up when I asked him what movie we were going to watch on Saturday night. He said it really loudly, and I'm sure other people heard it. At lunch, he told me just to eat a salad because of my "big legs." And I know some of the other football players and their girlfriends heard him say that because one of those senior girls snickered. I'm sure it was at me. I'd rather eat with Paige, Hannah, and Mia anyway, but Caleb won't let me. When we were getting ready to leave the cafeteria for fourth period, Mr. Caldwell came over to us and said, "Elly, your dress attire is not school-appropriate. Please go to my office, call home, ask someone to bring you a change of clothing, and wait there until they do." I'd never been sent to the office before. I'd never been in trouble with a principal or assistant principal before.

Before I left that morning, Mom had fussed about the clothes thing; and now, she was going to get the satisfaction of saying, "I told you so." Mom wasn't happy when she got to school; she made that very clear to me. That evening, she fixed a really nice dinner with chocolate cake for dessert. I felt so guilty about eating the cake that after dinner, I went to the bathroom and made myself throw up. I'm going to try to lose at least two or three pounds by this weekend to show Caleb I'm serious about looking the way he wants me to.

On Tuesday, at school, Caleb got mad at me again. In A.P. History on Monday, Mr. Martin had asked us to write down on a piece of paper who we wanted to work with on projects he was going to assign. Of course, I wrote down Caleb's name. Mr. Martin had said we were going to start the year by studying the Colonial Era, and he was going to assign us a series of projects. Two or three times a week, different two-person groups would present lessons to the class on some historical situation that helped lead to the Revolutionary War, and even the Civil War. He said we would, in effect, be teaching the class that day as part of the period. I really liked the idea of that since I want to be an elementary school teacher.

But on Tuesday, when Mr. Martin assigned topics, he paired me with Leigh, who I barely know and who used to date Caleb. He got so mad at me after class, and he called me a "lying bitch" when I told him that I had put his name down when Mr. Martin asked who we wanted to work with. Before lunch started, I went back to Mr. Martin's room and asked him why I was working with Leigh. He said he had asked us to write down who we wanted to work with so that he could give us somebody else to work with, and that it would be good for us to get to know other people better and get us "out of our comfort zones." Doing so would also likely make for better presentations. I told all that to Caleb at lunch, and he still didn't believe me.

Caleb was in a really bad mood after the football game on Friday night. He sat on the bench the whole night, and didn't get to play at all. The guy who replaced him, I think his name is Antonio, threw a bunch of touchdown passes, and the crowd just went crazy all night. We won by a lot of points, I don't remember how many... football is such a ridiculous sport. Why do you get six points, or is it seven, when you score one touchdown?

Caleb barely spoke to me at all when we met with some of the other juniors and seniors and their girlfriends for pizza. He kept complaining about Antonio's passing and how, if he had been the quarterback, we would have scored even more points. I just kept my mouth shut when he was ranting on and on. He would have criticized me anyway, no matter what I would have said.

On Saturday night, about a half-hour before he was supposed to pick me up for our date, he texted me—he didn't even bother to call—that something had come up and we wouldn't be going out that night. At first, my feelings were hurt that he would stand me up after I had spent all that time getting ready to look nice for him. I had also wanted to tell him that I had lost two pounds this week. But then I was really glad that I didn't have to go out with him. All he does anymore is yell at me and criticize how I look and dress. I've got to get up enough courage to break up with him. I don't care how much my parents like him.

CHAPTER SEVEN

MARCUS

On the second game of the season, I only played four snaps on offense the entire night. All four were on third and long downs, and Antonio threw all four of those passes in the direction of Tito or Matthew. It was like I'm not even part of the offense anymore. Coach Dell had told me he was going to get me on the field some by letting me be the extra cornerback on sure passing downs, and I did play five or six downs in that situation.

But every time I tried to cover the receiver, it just didn't feel natural to be on defense. The other team's receiver burned me three times for long gains. I just couldn't keep up with him. It's so obvious that I can't run as fast as I used to. I did play on all the kickoffs, and there were a lot of them because Antonio kept throwing touchdowns to Tito and Matthew. I was glad for the team; but to be honest, I'm really miserable sitting on the bench. I feel left out of things.

Kylee tried to boost my spirits after the game, and her doing that helped a little. She means so much to me. I never thought any girl would, but she sincerely cares about how I'm doing. She asked if I wanted for us to join some of the other juniors and seniors for pizza after the game, but I said no. I just wanted to go home and call Joshua at college. He knows what it's like to play football and have a bad game.

"Just try to be a good teammate," he said. "Finish out the year, and be positive with Coach Dell and the other coaches and your teammates. Next summer, you can decide whether or not to play football again. You might even want to think about doing another fall sport... maybe cross country? You should also focus on doing really well in your classes."

I have been doing that, especially in my favorite class, A.P. History. The other day, Mr. Martin announced that we would be doing a lot of two-person presentations this year, and he paired me up with Luke. You know, I've been in classes with him since middle school, but I've never really talked to him much or tried to get to know him. Martin gave us our topic: the influence of religion on white people's feelings on slavery before the Revolutionary War. Now, that's an assignment I can get into. The bigotry of most whites, no matter how religious they were, toward my ancestors was pathetic during that time period.

When Luke and I started to research the topic, I figured he would be all defensive about white racial prejudice. But he was as angry about it as I was, and it wasn't an act on his part. I had to ask him why; and he said that all his life, upper-class white people had looked down on him, and he was pretty sure that people back then had looked down on lower-class whites and despised them, just like they did the black slaves. After all, he said, the Founding Fathers didn't want poor whites having a say in things any more than they wanted the slaves to. That the poor whites obviously had it better than the slaves did; but they couldn't vote either, just like the blacks, and the system was rigged against both racial groups. That a poor white had only a slightly better chance of getting out of his poverty-stricken state than a free black did, and the black slave was doomed no matter what.

Wow, the dude was really worked up about this thing! Before I knew it, we were talking about all kinds of things that had to do with the assigned topic, and all kinds of other things as well. Luke's a really interesting guy. I've spent so much time around the "popular" kids, and all of them are just like me; we all come from middle- or upper-class neighborhoods. I've never even bothered to get to know guys like Luke. I mean, I'm not knocking him by calling him lower-class... it's just a fact. You can tell it by the clothes he wears and that old Ford pickup he drives. Maybe I shouldn't have asked him this, but I've seen people like Caleb and Matthew make fun of him behind his back in some of our classes. He must have heard those remarks about him being "poor white trash." So, I asked him if he had heard them, and if he ever thought about going off on any of those guys.

"Of course, I heard what they said," said Luke. "But I never wanted to give them the satisfaction of thinking they had gotten under my skin. I've used that crap to motivate me."

I had to ask him how.

"I've got a chip on my shoulder because of people like Caleb," he said. "Every time somebody like him puts me down, I use it to motivate myself to do better. One day, I will be somebody. Caleb is an SOB now, and he'll be an SOB his whole life. Him having advantages now won't ever change that."

I laughed out loud when he said that, and he grinned at me. Martin then snapped at us to get back to work. And, man, did we. We put together this fantastic PowerPoint called "How Whites Used Religion to Both Justify and Attack Slavery Pre-Revolutionary War." I mean, the title was too long, but we didn't know what else to call it.

Luke and I put on this awesome presentation on Friday of that week, and we both ripped into everything that we thought was wrong with the white aristocracy during that time period, but we also covered the beginning of the abolitionist movement. After we were done, Mr. Martin raved and raved about our presentation, and announced to the class that that kind of effort was what he expected out of everyone. I didn't have a good week on the football field, but I was a real stud in the history classroom.

CHAPTER EIGHT

MIA

My father arranged for me to have a date with Miguel on Saturday night. I really didn't want to go, but I did. I haven't had a date or really done anything but study or work since Luke and I broke up.

Mama did the strangest thing before Miguel came to pick me up. When I was getting ready, she came to my room and said she had been saving money on the side and had bought me a cell phone. I had been needing one for the longest time. I'm tired of borrowing other girls' phones when I've needed to contact Mama during the day about something. My father and I are barely talking at all, so there's definitely no need to call him.

During the date, I was super glad I had that phone. When Miguel picked me up, I admit it was nice. He is definitely good-looking and a charmer with the way he complimented how I looked. He's a sophomore at the local college, so he's three years older than I am, which was more than a little uncomfortable. I had a lot of questions about what he's majoring in and why (business, because he feels it would prepare him for just about anything), and how hard college was (it's not all that hard).

We ate dinner at a really nice restaurant, much nicer than any place I've ever been to before. And I have to admit that going to someplace like that was glamorous. If he had taken me home after that, I might have considered going out with him again. He's not a great conversationalist, but I need to see what other guys are like after only ever going out with Luke.

When we were finished eating, Miguel told me that there was a party at the house of one of his friends, and he wanted us to drop by and meet some of the people he hangs with… and that maybe I could make some new friends there. It all seemed so innocent, so I said yes. When we got there, there were four other couples there, and it was pretty obvious that probably everybody had been drinking pretty heavily—liquor bottles were everywhere. Miguel asked me if I would like for him to make me a mixed drink of some kind, and he gave me all these choices. I told him no thanks. I've never drunk alcohol before.

Then he asked me if I would like some punch, so I said yes. It didn't taste right, but I drank it all; then I realized it had been spiked. How could I have been so naïve? I told Miguel that I didn't appreciate his sense of humor. His response was to offer me some more punch, that I "would get used to the taste," and that I "needed to loosen up some and really experience college life."

He had been drinking non-stop since we arrived, and his speech was already a little slurred. Why would he think that a drunk college sophomore would be appealing to me—even if he were 100-percent Hispanic and the ideal man that my father had chosen for me? It was about then that I had noticed that several of the couples had wandered off somewhere; and Miguel said, "I have a room reserved for us. Let's go." I had been stupid about the punch, but I'm not naïve about what he was suggesting we should go do.

"I need to go to the restroom and get ready. Is that okay?"

And he laughed this fake sexy laugh and said, "Now you're seeing things my way. See you soon."

I went to the bathroom and immediately called Mama and told her about Miguel's "offer," and that she needed to come pick me up right now. I had seen a gas station about a half-mile from the house, and I told her that I would meet her there. I slipped out the back door right after the phone call, and walked as fast as I could to the station.

When the car arrived, I was surprised to see both Mama and my father in it. It was then that I realized how scared I had been about Miguel's "offer," and seeing my father made me so furious.

"Are you alright?" asked Mama. "Did Miguel..." Her voice trailed off.

"No, I'm not all right. And no, Miguel didn't. But it was no thanks to you, father," I said and looked straight at him.

"Don't take that tone with me," he said.

"And don't you try to set me up with any more sons of your friends," I said. "That is, unless you want me to get pregnant while I'm still in high school. Is that your plan? Do you want to go back and drop me off at Miguel's bedroom? I'm sure he'll forgive me for running out on him."

Nobody said a word all the way home after that little exchange. I went straight to my room when we got home; and once again, I heard Mama and my father arguing. My head was hurting from the punch, or maybe it was from all the anger I felt inside. Luke never treated me with a lack of respect.

Later in the evening, Mama came to my room; and she said she was proud of me and my quick thinking, and that she was so glad that she had bought me that cell phone. I started crying, and we just held each other for several minutes.

I almost called Luke after she left. I miss our late-night conversations so much.

HOMECOMING WEEKEND

CHAPTER NINE

LUKE

Last week, I got up enough courage to ask out a girl, Amber. She transferred to my school a while back, and has been in a bunch of my classes. She's pretty and smart, and I hadn't seen her with any guys this year; so I thought, why not see if she might be interested in going out with me? She's my third-period Advanced Chemistry lab partner, so I've gotten to know her a little bit.

When I asked her out for coffee last Friday night, she got this surprised look on her face, hesitated a little, then finally said okay. I don't know much about girls, but I think all that was a bad sign—it had to have been. I only have two pairs of dress pants, which is one more than what I had when I lived with Mom and Dad. I wore the tan khakis and a blue shirt; I just wanted to make a good impression when I met her folks to pick her up at 7. Her dad is a retired Marine, and Amber said later that he met her mom when he was overseas, in Asia. Her dad acted kind of cold to me, and her mom didn't say too much, either. You mean they weren't impressed that I picked up their daughter in a 20-year-old Ford pickup? Not much I can do about that.

We talked about some pretty interesting stuff. Amber said that she hates that "All Asians are so smart" stereotype, and that she has to work just as hard as everybody else to make good grades. On the other hand, her mom puts more pressure on her than her dad does to make an *A* in every subject. Her mom expects her to be in the top 10 of the class, and perhaps even make valedictorian. But that's not possible because "Everybody knows that Mia has that locked up," said Amber.

She got this weird look on her face when she said that, then said, "I'm sorry I brought up Mia."

I told her that was okay; Mia and I were over, and it was time for me to move on. Amber and I ran out of things to say around 8:30, and I took her home before 9. I'm not going to ask her out again—she would probably say no. There's nothing wrong with her. There was just no *magic*. You know what I mean?

This weekend was Homecoming; and my Yearbook teacher, Ms. Hawk, assigned Elly and me to do our usual thing of covering the big Homecoming football game on Friday night. That Friday, in Yearbook class, Elly explained that Caleb had told her she had to tell me if I so much as accidentally brushed up against her later that night, he would "deal" with me. I'm sure Elly verbally edited out what Caleb had really said to her.

Elly came to her front door when I arrived to pick her up. That was good because having to talk to two foul fathers in a week's time was not something I wanted to deal with. Elly didn't say anything when I picked her up; then after we had been driving for about two minutes, she just started crying. I pulled the truck over and asked what the matter was.

"I'm really sorry for talking to you the way I did in Yearbook today," she said, still sobbing. "I'm scared of Caleb. I'm scared of what he might do to me. I'm scared of what he might do to you or anybody, boy or girl, even if what we're doing is innocent. He's an awful person."

"Why are you still with him, Elly?" I said. "You're one of the smartest girls I've ever met. You've got a great personality, you're pretty. You've got a great future. Caleb's a loser. You can do better."

I swear, I hate Caleb; and I almost said that, too. Then all these feelings I've had for her the whole time I've known her, except when Mia and I were dating, just started building up inside. And I almost told her how I felt about her.

"Please just take me home," she said. "I'll tell Ms. Hawk I got sick before the game and couldn't take pictures."

"No, Elly, we've got to go to the game," I said. "I've got to have these pictures for my Homecoming game spread. Why don't you take the pictures for the first half, and I'll take you home at halftime? I don't want to spend the whole night at the football game, either."

She stopped crying, then said she would text Caleb at halftime and tell him that she had gotten sick, and was going home and wouldn't be able to make their date after the game. All in all, it was a good plan. I got the pictures, she avoided a late night with Caleb, and neither one of us had to sit in the bleachers for like three hours. Although, I admit I got at least a little bit of pleasure watching Caleb either riding the bench or pacing back and forth on the sidelines all night, having no chance to get in the game. How many college scouts are coming to talk to you now, Mr. Future NFL Superstar?

When Elly and I left the game at halftime, we talked all the way to her house. She kept thanking me for being "such a sweet guy," then we talked about our favorite classes. It's Yearbook and English for both of us, and neither one of us can stand Advanced Chem. It was just great. Maybe I shouldn't have said what I did when I dropped her off. But I'm glad I did.

CHAPTER TEN

ELLY

I was shocked last Friday night when Luke asked me to go out with him. I mean, he knows that Caleb and I are dating. I had felt so depressed when he came to pick me up for us to cover the Homecoming game for Yearbook. During the drive, I had told him to take me home because I was so worn out and upset about Caleb, plus everything else. I've never felt so much stress in my entire life, what with Caleb and all these hard classes. I've got a *B* average in two classes, and a *C* in Chemistry. I've never made grades that low.

Luke talked me into staying through halftime, and I was glad we did. I didn't want to disappoint Ms. Hawk and not take some good photos for Luke's Yearbook spread. On the way home, Luke and I talked and talked. It felt so good to actually enjoy being around a guy for a change. I was flattered when he asked me out, and I hope his feelings weren't hurt. But Caleb would absolutely go off on Luke—and me—if he found out that Luke had even asked me out.

When I got home, I called Paige and told her that Luke had asked me out. The first thing she said was, "I hope you said yes."

"I can't go out with Luke. Caleb and I are together," I said.

Paige laughed out loud at that, then asked me what planet was I living on... that Mary had been talking for weeks about how pretty Caleb's girlfriend from Jefferson High School was, and that she had seen them together at his parents' lake house over the summer. I told her that Mary was wrong about all that; but in my heart, I knew that what Paige said was almost certainly true.

"I can understand why you wouldn't want to go out with Luke," Paige continued. "No girl in her right mind would want to go out with a sweet, kind guy who has had a crush on her for like forever. Why would she choose a guy like that over a guy who treats her like dirt, cheats on her, and is constantly criticizing her looks and weight and everything about her? Your decision makes perfect sense to me, Elly."

I told her that I didn't appreciate her sarcasm. I almost hung up on her, but didn't. I needed to talk to either her or Mia about all this stuff, and I sure can't call Mia and ask her whether I should break up with Caleb and go out with Luke.

"My parents think Caleb is awesome," I said next.

"Well, maybe your parents would like to be Caleb's BFFs," said Paige.

"That's not funny," I said.

"Look, suppose you went out with Luke, and suppose you two really got into each other. What if you two fell in love one day? What would be so bad about that? A lot of girls think guys like Luke aren't exciting... aren't worth their time. And they fall for these perfect jerks who break their hearts over and over. Yeah, keep on going out with Caleb, and see what that brings ya."

"I turned Luke down," was all I could think to say, then I actually hung up on her. I just tried to put the whole thing out of my mind, but I tossed and turned all night and hardly got any sleep. What if Paige were right about Caleb cheating on me? Who am I fooling? She is right. But I just can't fall for Luke. He's just not... I don't know. Dad doesn't like him.

I spent all of Saturday morning trying to get caught up on schoolwork; but I only got my reading done for English and history, and didn't even start on the Algebra II and Advanced

Chemistry stuff. Saturday afternoon, Mom and I spent a lot of time fussing over my makeup and hair. It was really nice to have some time with her, except when she kept going on and on about how good-looking Caleb is, how we're a great match, and how Caleb's mom is always raving about how glad she is about us being a couple.

On Saturday night, Caleb picked me up, then said he had to go pick up Mary and Matthew because all of us were going together. I didn't even know that Mary and Matthew are a thing. I could care less, except that Matthew is my ex; and Caleb should have asked me how I felt about doubling with them. That really hurt my feelings.

On the way to the dance, all Caleb talked about was how unfair Coach Dell had been to him after the game Friday night, and how he was thinking about quitting the team. That he could "walk on" at some "big-time" college and show Dell how wrong he was about benching him. What does "walk on" even mean? Who cares, I don't even want to know.

The Homecoming setting was really nice. It was in the gym and the theme was "Under the Sea," with palm trees, fishing nets, life preservers, and painted fish. There was also this miniature drive-in movie setup with cardboard cars where couples could sit and watch real movies like *Hairspray*, *Grease*, and *High School Musical*. Caleb basically ignored me once we got there, mostly talking to the other football players and flirting with every girl who walked past him.

We hadn't even been there for 20 minutes when he said he and Matthew had to go out to the car and get something. They were gone for like 45 minutes, and I was scared to leave where he left me because he gets so mad so easily over just about anything. Then Mr. Caldwell came up to me and said, "Caleb will not be returning to the dance due to breaking school policy. Do you need to call your parents for a ride home?"

A few minutes later, Mary came over and said that Matthew had just texted her and said that Caldwell had caught him and Caleb trying to bring alcohol into the building. They had gotten kicked out of the dance and suspended for a week. Mary said she was going to hang around at the dance; I bet she tried to find the cutest guy there without a date.

I called Mom and told her what happened, and to come pick me up. She needs to know what the real Caleb is like.

CHAPTER ELEVEN

MARCUS

I have to say, I was impressed with the way Antonio ran the offense in the Homecoming game on Friday night. His arm was like a cannon when Matthew and Tito would go deep, and he had touch when he had to dump the ball off to a running back coming out of the backfield. We were ahead 28-0 at halftime. Matthew and Tito had each caught a pair of touchdown passes.

I even helped the team a little. On 3rd and 12 in the second quarter, I caught a 15-yarder which set up a bomb to Tito two plays later. Later, I was the nickelback on a 3rd and 11, and I tipped away a pass intended for one of their receivers. Both times, Coach Dell praised me like crazy when I came back to the bench. I really appreciated that. At least I feel more a part of things than when I first lost my starting job. But the bench was where I spent most of the night until the fourth quarter, when we were up 42-0. Coach Dell put the scrubs in, including me and Caleb, of course.

I was shocked when Caleb called the first play in the huddle; he told me to go long. I mean, you don't throw long passes, man. You don't throw passes, period, when you're up big against a team. It's poor sportsmanship. Besides, it's bulletin-board material the next time you play a team. They're all out to get you because you dissed them and ran up the score. Hector, our junior center, asked Caleb if he were sure that Dell had called a pass. Caleb got all up in his face, and told him to do as he was told and get up to the line. I mean, Caleb was just ballistic.

I went deep like he told me; and pretty much like the old days when we were both starters, he sailed the ball way over my head. The next thing I knew, Coach Dell called a timeout and was screaming at Caleb and the entire offense. It didn't take him long to find out the pass play was Caleb's idea and nobody else's. Nobody on the team can stand Caleb; he's such a prima donna. Nobody was going to take the fall for him.

Coach Dell told Caleb to take his helmet off and go sit on the bench, that he was through for the night and that he would deal with him later after the game. I went to sit down and saw Caleb heading for the locker room against Dell's orders. When we all got back to the locker room after the game, Caleb was gone. I found out later that he had quit the team. Good. He won't be missed.

On Saturday night, I was all set to take Kylee out to dinner and to the Homecoming dance, but she told me after the game on Friday to break the dinner reservations—she had decided to cook a really nice dinner for us at her house. I was just shocked when she said that… that she would go through all this effort to cook for me. The meal was just great. We ate by candlelight on the dinner table, and her parents stayed downstairs in the rec room. She made a prime rib—medium rare—for me with potato croquettes and a vegetable medley, plus key lime pie for dessert. I raved about everything; but mostly, I told her I was sincerely touched that she would do that for me. Not many girls would spend hours cooking for a guy, especially when they had originally planned to go out to a nice restaurant.

The dance was great. I especially liked the drive-in part with old movies being shown while couples could sit in these fake cars. We took a break from dancing and socializing, and just sat and watched a movie together for about half an hour.

I told Kylee how much she means to me, and how I was so glad that she gave me a second chance. She gave me a super long kiss after I said that.

On Monday, in U.S. History, Luke and I started work on our second project together, "What if America Had Lost the War of 1812?" We came up with the idea together, and Mr. Martin just went on and on about how it was a great idea for a presentation to the class. Luke speculated that there wouldn't have been a Civil War if England had beaten us in 1812. The possibility of that happening and how it would have affected Jim Crow and everything else was just awesome for Luke and me to try to figure out.

I told Luke that I had decided for sure not to play football in my senior year, and he said that I ought to go run cross country, that he really likes it a lot... doing all that running would get me ready for basketball season. That got me to thinking that, yeah, all that going up and down hills and stuff would be great for basketball. Coach Henson runs us all the time.

I also asked him what he thought about me majoring in history, and maybe working at a museum or doing some sort of historical interpretation job. He said I would be great at that, and that he always learned a lot about history when we working on projects and stuff. Luke's an okay dude. I would never have learned that if Martin hadn't paired us up.

CHAPTER TWELVE

MIA

Two weeks ago, I got nominated for the Homecoming court again. My first thought was that I was not going to let my father know because I didn't want him escorting me out onto the field at halftime. My second thought was that being there was going to waste at least two or three hours of my time. I was either going to lose money from babysitting, or lose time from studying, or both.

I am so stressed out from studying all the time. I'm just exhausted. It's not that the college and advanced courses are so hard; it's just that there are so many of them, and they all require a lot of either reading, research, or writing papers. I'm not worried about getting an *A* in all of the classes. I'm worried about getting enough sleep to function the next day.

To make things even more complicated, a guy asked me out to Homecoming. His name is Hector, he transferred to the school this year, and he's in my afternoon English Honors class. I barely know him. He's nice enough; but he's Hispanic, and when he asked me, I almost turned him down immediately because my father would probably like the fact that I might go out with a Hispanic guy. But then I realized that rejecting him because of that would be just as bad as my father shunning Luke because he is white and lower-class.

I was so confused about what to do, and so surprised

about Hector asking me out that I started stuttering, which I never do. I finally decided to just tell him the truth: that I hadn't expected anyone to ask me out to Homecoming, and I didn't have a thing to wear, and could I just get back to him in a few days?

He said, "You're one of the most beautiful girls in the school. I figured that you'd turn me down because a bunch of guys had already asked you out."

It was sweet of him to say that, but I don't really think of myself as beautiful. I haven't worn any makeup since the last time Luke and I went out; and on most days, I go off to school with my hair in a ponytail or in a bun and wearing the same old pair of jeans. It's not that I don't care about how I look; it's just that I don't have time to spend in front of a mirror.

There's another reason why I didn't want to go. Money has gotten tighter this year. My father lost his Saturday janitor job because of cutbacks. His construction boss cut back on all the workers' hours during the week because there hasn't been that much work to do. I think that that's another reason my parents have been arguing more. They both feel the stress of less money coming in. For sure, I couldn't ask Mama to buy me a Homecoming dress.

I told her about Hector asking me, and she said she could make me a dress the weekend before Homecoming; and to go ahead and tell him yes. So I did. It would probably do me good to not be studying or working all the time... at least, that was how I rationalized things.

Actually, Hector and I had a pretty good time. He took me out to a restaurant before the dance, and we got to know each other a little. His grandparents immigrated from Cuba right before Castro took over, and made sure that Hector's father got a college education. His dad is a policeman, and his mom is a high school Spanish teacher in the adjoining county, so they are doing pretty well... a lot better than my family is. Hector is not sure what he's going to do for a career; he said he'd make up his mind after the first two years of college. I can understand that; not everyone knows what they're going to do when they're juniors in high school.

Homecoming was nice, but we didn't do much dancing. Hector said he had turned his ankle during the football game on Friday night. I didn't even know he played football until he told me. I guess I don't pay that much attention to what's going on at school outside of class... maybe I should. But high school just seems so temporary, and all the drama that's always going on seems so pointless and immature. I mean, who's going to care in five years if some girl or guy dissed each other on social media on Tuesday night? Our high school years shouldn't define who we are as people.

I admit that I looked around to see what the other girls were wearing. It must be nice to be able to afford clothes that you might only wear once or twice. But I don't feel deprived because I don't have any really nice clothes. So what? If my dreams work out the way I hope they will, one day I won't have to deal with this constant fear of never having enough money to just get by.

When Hector took me home, he gave me a kiss and said the required, "I had a really good time." It was the first time anybody had kissed me since Luke had right before my father broke us up. Will I go out with him again? Maybe, I don't know. It just doesn't matter, one way or the other.

GOOD GRADES,
BAD GRADES

CHAPTER THIRTEEN

LUKE

My first nine weeks' grades weren't what I hoped they would be. I'm actually studying and trying harder than I ever have before, but these eleventh-grade classes are a lot harder than any I've ever taken. So my grades have been pretty much like they always have been—everything from good to average to awful. I had an *A* in U.S. History, and a big reason for that were the projects that Marcus and I did on slavery and religion, plus the one on the War of 1812.

I got a *B* in English because I didn't do any of the writing prompts that Ms. Roche assigned for homework. I know she's frustrated with me because I won't do the prompts to help us prepare for the state tests. One day before class, she asked me why I wouldn't do them because I was such a "good writer." And I told her that was precisely the reason I wasn't doing those stupid prompts: that they were juvenile and silly. I mean, the last two prompts were "Why You Should Not Set Your Aims Too Low" and "Do You Think Having a Positive Attitude is Important?"

Mm, should I take the position that setting my aims and goals in life really low would be the right thing? Should I take the position that a sucky attitude leads to a successful life? I asked Ms. Roche why should I waste an hour of my time after school doing such ridiculous crap. I'm stressed out all the time. I don't get home from cross country until nearly 7. I've got to eat something, and then I've got like four hours of homework to do. I asked her if I should neglect my remedial math class, where I have a high *F* and have got to bring it up to a low *D*. Or do I neglect the Chemistry class, where I have a low *D* and am desperately trying to keep the grade from becoming a high *F*?

She didn't really have an answer for that, except to say that these were the prompts "handed down by the state for the state tests," and it was "crucial" that we all did well. I told her we were an honors class, and nobody in there was in danger of failing the English state test. And she knew that. Why couldn't we write about something that was more relevant to our lives? I don't know for sure, but I think she's frustrated about how much emphasis she has to place on the state tests— that she'd like to tell us that they're a bunch of crap.

Then there's Spanish III class, and the *C*- average that's got future *D* written all over it. The other day, we were taking turns reading out loud; and the first word of my sentence started with *ahora*. Ms. Young interrupted me as soon as I started. "Luke, it's not pronounced 'A-whore-uh'." Man, she was mad. The class erupted in laughter. Then she added, "The letter *h* should be like good children: seen but not heard." That last remark really hurt. I wasn't intentionally trying to screw up.

She asked me to read some more, and the next sentence started off with *me llamo*. Once again, she interrupted me. "Luke, it's not 'me-lame-o'; it's 'may yamo'." And again, everybody in class was laughing at me. I'm not trying to be stupid; this stuff is hard to pronounce.

Ms. Young then went on about the importance of the preterit and imperfect tenses. She said, "The preterit tells us specifically when an action took place. The imperfect tells us in general when an action took place." How the heck are we supposed to tell whether the speaker is being general or definite when I can barely make out what he's saying in the first place? I'm studying those new vocabulary words every night; but then we'll have a whole new set the next night, and it seems like I'd then forget about half the words I *learned* the night before.

The bad stuff continued when Ms. Whitney called me to the guidance office. I figured it had to be about whether I was "eligible for special services in math." Sure enough, that was it. I knew that Granddaddy had to go to school for a meeting with my math teacher, Mrs. Roberts, and Ms. Whitney as part of the "process" based on my Child Study. I had taken a standardized math test a couple of weeks ago, and I felt like I scored really bad on it... and from the way she started our talk, I must have.

"Everyone has weaknesses, and math is yours, Luke. You having a collaborative teacher to help you in math will be a very good thing and not put a label on you. I know you're worried about that."

Yep, it sure won't be embarrassing when it's time to do something about the stupid kids. When Mrs. Roberts motions for Mrs. Cary to take the seven dumbest kids in remedial math, including me, to the special ed office for "extra help," every single person in class is going to think, "There go all the lucky kids. I sure wish I could be going with them. Oh my, oh yes, it must be wonderful to be so stupid in a remedial math class."

The best thing that happened to me all of last week was getting to go run for miles on a national forest trail as part of cross country practice. It felt so, the word is *freeing*, to be outside and just running and running past trees, creeks, and mountainsides—those things that I love so much. It was almost as good as going off into the mountains to hunt and fish.

One day, I went off the main trail onto a spur to see if the wild grapes I know that grow there were ripe. They were, too. I pulled off a cluster to eat as I ran. When I got back on the main trail, I saw Leigh sitting on a rock. She said she had turned her ankle, and was in pain. I found a stout walking stick for her to use to help keep the weight off her ankle. She asked me not to run off and leave her. She said she was afraid that she would have to walk out by herself in the dark.

I said I would walk with her. I could tell she'd never been out in the forest before. She kept asking if there were bears and mountain lions around. I said that mountain lions had been extinct for over 150 years in our state, and that bears are usually only a threat if humans accidentally separate a sow from her cubs. About an hour later, a couple of our teammates came looking for us. They said Coach Guthridge figured that something must have happened. It was nice walking and talking with her. I had always assumed she was an airhead because she used to date Caleb. But she's not.

CHAPTER FOURTEEN

ELLY

I'm stressed out over my grades, my relationship with Caleb, and having to explain to my mom that I need to lose more weight. I've lost four more pounds, which I thought would satisfy Caleb, but he said my legs are still too big. I haven't been this thin since seventh grade, and all my clothes are too loose. Mom keeps telling me not to lose any more weight, and I keep telling her that I have to get thinner. I haven't told her that Caleb is telling me to. If I did that, she'd probably think me losing more weight was a great idea. She likes him so much, she thinks he's soooo perfect.

I've made myself throw up four times in the past two weeks, all because Mom served some kind of chocolate dessert that I shouldn't have eaten. And she shouldn't have served it. Paige and Mia have both told me I'm too thin and don't look like myself. Mia even asked me, privately, if I was making myself throw up. She said she had read about the symptoms. Who does she think she is to be saying something like that? Just because she wants to be a doctor doesn't make her an expert. I am not bulimic like she sort of hinted at. I just need to lose a few more pounds, that's all.

My grades are just adding to the stress. I've got this burning sensation in my stomach; I know it's from worrying about my grades. I made a *B* average in Algebra II and a *C* in Advanced

Chemistry for the nine weeks. Chemistry is absolutely the worst and most boring class I've ever taken... it's the hardest, too. That stuff about valence electrons, electron dot structures, and all those laws and principles... it's just awful. Everything else is an *A*, but I've never had a *C* in anything for a grading period, except for those stupid phys ed and health classes... thank goodness I'm done taking them.

The only good thing that has happened to me lately was Caleb quitting the football team. He says he quit, but everybody else is saying he got kicked off. I could care less about how it happened. The good news is that I don't have go to any more football games and pretend like I care what's going on.

Caleb told me he would only be able to go out with me on Friday nights for the "next little while." He says he's got a lot of other things to take care of right now. Mary keeps telling me he's cheating on me. Paige and Mia have told me to break up with him. I can't do that. Things will get better between us, I know they will. I just have to lose a little more weight and stop doing things that make him mad.

I still haven't told anybody besides Paige that Luke asked me out. Not even the other day in history class, when my project partner, Leigh, started talking about Luke. We were supposed to be working on the Dred Scott Decision, but all Leigh wanted to talk about was how sweet Luke was to her when she turned her ankle during cross country practice. She said she knew that we were friends and worked together in Yearbook, and she wanted to know what kind of guy he was. She said she was maybe interested in him, which I just couldn't believe. I mean, she's always dated certain kinds of guys... those really popular guys, mostly the ones who play football or basketball, or live in my neighborhood or ones like it. Those kinds of guys—the ones who dress sharp and look great.

I know she used to date Caleb. That's made things a little awkward between us, or at least I thought it did, but the subject of Caleb never came up until she asked about Luke.

"I've dated a few guys who were just awful to be around, controlling and acting like they knew everything," she started off saying. "You know that type of guy."

I interrupted her when she said that, and I told her not to criticize Caleb.

"I didn't mention his name, but since you brought him up," she said, "he's the worst guy I've ever dated. I only went out with him the first time because he was so good-looking, the starting quarterback and all that. We were around each other all the time because I was a cheerleader then. Caleb's the worst mistake I've ever made. If you want to know the truth, I can't believe a girl as smart and pretty as you is still going out with him."

I started to argue with her again, but Mr. Martin must have figured we weren't talking about Dred Scott and told us "to stop yapping and get back to work." The next day, before first-period English, Leigh saw me in the hall and apologized about our argument. "You and Caleb are none of my business," she said. "But I'm thinking of trying to get to know Luke better, to sort of go through the talking stage with him. I just wanted to know what you think of him. He doesn't seem to be dating anybody."

I told her that Luke is a really sweet guy and that Mia had told me she was still not over him, but I thought Luke had moved on. Leigh asked if I knew where he hung out during lunch… that she never saw him in the cafeteria. I told her that he always went to the library.

"Alright," she said and smiled.

I just know she's going to turn on the charm with Luke, with that long blonde hair of hers and those long, perfect legs. All of a sudden, I felt all this jealousy toward her. Then all those feelings I have for Luke every now and then came over me. Just for the quickest moment or two, I was comparing Caleb and Luke in my head; and there's no question about who came out on top: Luke, by a landslide.

CHAPTER FIFTEEN

MARCUS

I absolutely rocked my report card for the nine weeks! Everything was an *A* except for a *B* in Honors Chemistry, which is absolutely the hardest class I've ever taken. Why is Le Chatelier's Principle the answer to everything? I don't understand. What does ionization energy have to do with anything? I mean, man, really?

Still, when I told Mom and Dad that they could go online and see my grades for the nine weeks, it was pretty sweet when they did. Dad gave me a high-five, and Mom was smiling big time. My favorite class is an elective: Mr. Wayne's American Conflicts. It's the best because we dig deep to see what the causes were behind the things that made history. What were the reasons for the Revolutionary War? What would have had to happen for there not to have been a Civil War? But also, might the Civil War have been inevitable? How did Eisenhower, Kennedy, Johnson, and Nixon all make blunders that had to do with the Vietnam War? I mean, who knew that history could be this interesting? I've got an *A*-plus in that class and Honors U.S. History with Mr. Martin, too. I'm definitely, definitely going to major in history at college.

The other day, I asked Mr. Wayne if I could read some more things that were history-related. He said if I wanted to read something every day that would be interesting, I should go to realclearhistory.com and see what events from the past were going to be covered for the day. One day, I read about Hitler's private secretary. Another day, I read about major instances of American corruption like Teapot Dome and Watergate. One of the best articles I read was about the ten most corrupt politicians in American history. This country has had some really greedy dudes.

Wayne also told me that I might want to ask my parents to get a subscription to *Smithsonian Magazine*. I went to Mrs. Kendel in the library to see if I could check out some old magazines and see what they were like, and she said yes. I read this fascinating story about the 1918 flu epidemic, and another issue had a story about the black migration from the South to the North. Maybe that's why we live where we do now, you know? Wouldn't it be great if I could work for the Smithsonian or some other museum, doing research, maybe giving lectures... working with high school classes or colleges? That would be cool.

I'm glad football season is over. I hate to say it, but I'm glad that we didn't make the playoffs. I'm glad, too, that I stuck it out for the whole season and didn't quit or get kicked off the team like Caleb did when I lost my starting position. It's not that I enjoyed losing the last game, but I just wanted to get in on a few practices with the basketball team before the season started.

I told Coach Dell that I wasn't going to play for the football team in my senior year, and he gave me a big compliment. "I'm going to miss working with you, Marcus. You've grown as a person and a teammate. I was planning on making you an offensive captain in your senior year."

I was shocked about the captain thing and told Dell. I told him I knew I wouldn't be a starter in my senior year, but that wasn't why I wasn't going to play. I said I wanted to work on my basketball skills and run cross country to build up my stamina for the basketball season.

"It's true that you probably wouldn't have been a starter in your senior year, Marcus," he said. "But you likely would have been a captain because of your leadership abilities. You've come a long way since you were a freshman when your attitude... well, it left something to be desired."

He went on to say that being a captain was also about bringing "intangibles" to the team, and being a leader and role model. "You took your demotion to the bench like a man," he said. "That's leadership, too."

I really appreciated all that Dell said, and I told him that. But he and I both know that it's time for me to move on. This week, I got to practice all five days with the basketball team. It was awesome to be back with the guys, especially Quintin, our senior point guard. I felt we've really worked well together the past two years as the starting guards, and I felt like we were clicking pretty good all week in practice.

But on Friday after practice, Coach Henson asked me if I had time to talk to him before I drove home. I said I did. I had been meaning to ask him if I could work at the point guard position during games when Quintin was taking a blow. I'm now up to 6'6". Can you imagine how I would absolutely destroy on both defense and offense all those 6'2" and under point guards in our league?

I was just getting ready to ask Coach Henson about that when he said he wanted to get straight to the point. "Marcus, I want you to know that you're still going to start this year, but it's going to be at small forward instead of shooting guard."

I was shocked when he said that, and I asked him why.

"Because, Marcus, you've lost a step or two since your leg injury," he said. "You don't have that explosiveness off the dribble. I think you'd match up better against other teams' small forwards. Your outside shooting is as good as ever, if not better. And after a couple of threes early in the game, you could slash to the basket. It's best for the team and for you to change positions."

It hurt a little when he said that, but I'll just have to adjust. He was right. I'm still not back to what I was. Maybe I never will be.

CHAPTER SIXTEEN

MIA

I got an *A* on all my college and high school classes. I expected that of myself. But what I didn't expect was how hard I would have to work to make those good grades. Every night, day after day, it was the same thing. I come home, go to my room, read assignments, do homework or write papers until around 7:00, get something quick and bland to eat, then go back to my room and work until close to midnight. Then I get up at 6 and finish up last night's work before starting the whole blame thing all over again.

A couple of weeks ago, it occurred to me that this could be my life for my last two years of high school, four years of college, and all those years in medical school. It was depressing to think about. But I can do this thing. I can make my dreams of becoming a pediatrician come true.

But what kind of life will I lead? I want to marry one day and have at least two kids, maybe three; have a loving, kind man, a life partner who treats me as an equal. I was lucky to have a boy like Luke when I was really young, but my father took that away from me. When will I have time to meet guys and explore relationships and make wise decisions... fall in love with somebody? I just have this deep feeling that Luke and I would have fallen in love one day if we had been given half a chance.

I haven't heard from Hector since we went out a couple weeks ago. There were no calls, no texts; just a few quick nods when I would pass him in the hall, just a few random hellos when we would see each other in the cafeteria. In the past, I would hear my girlfriends complaining and agonizing that somebody hadn't called or texted since they went out, and what that all meant. Then they would ask the other girls and me what we thought about the situation, and analyze every little word or action between them and the guy. I always thought that when girls put themselves through that, they were being pathetic. Now I'm acting the same way.

I thought about sending Hector a text to see if he wanted to go out for coffee one day after school. I could use some time out of my room. But for years, Mama has told me over and over not to be forward with boys. Finally, I decided that I was going to do what I wanted. The way she and my father have been arguing for months, it's clear that she doesn't know everything about how to pick a man.

So, I texted Hector about hanging out. He didn't text back. The next day, when I got to school from college, he came up to me after I got out of the lunch line. He said he was surprised to hear from me, that I didn't seem to have had that good of a time when we went to Homecoming, and that he had heard I was still hung up on some other guy I used to date.

Maybe I am still hung up on Luke. Who am I fooling? I know that I am. But I can still talk to other guys while I'm sorting through all these feelings. So I said to Hector, "I just wanted to meet you for coffee, to talk, get to know you a little better… no big deal."

"I'm too busy this week" was what he said. "I'll get back to you maybe next week."

What's that supposed to mean? Maybe if he's bored and doesn't have anything else to do, he'll give me a call or text? Then something else occurred to me. Maybe he was telling the truth that he got the impression that I wasn't interested in him. Or maybe he didn't like the fact that I made the next move by texting him. Maybe he's one of those traditional guys who don't like it when girls make the suggestion for them to meet. Who knows how to deal with guys, anyway? They are so insecure.

Really, though, my guy problems are nothing compared to those of other people, like Elly, for instance. Paige told me the other day that she is really worried about Elly. I am, too. I'm convinced that Elly is binging and purging. She looks awful: thin with shadows under her eyes. She barely eats anything when she's in the cafeteria. I know; I've watched her when she's sitting beside Caleb at the jock table. Even when she does eat something, says Paige, Elly obsesses that she is eating too much and how fat she looks.

Paige suggested that me, her, Kylee, and Camila get together for a sleepover at Paige's house this Saturday, and have a real strong talk with Elly about how concerned we are… an intervention is what it's called. Paige said, "Saturdays are the nights that Caleb goes out with his 'other girlfriend,' so Elly will be free then."

Her voice was just dripping with sarcasm when she said that. I don't blame her for being concerned. Elly needs some help. She needs it now—before she really messes herself up further. I told Paige I would be there for sure.

RELATIONSHIPS BEGIN:
RELATIONSHIPS END

CHAPTER SEVENTEEN

LUKE

The other day, during lunch, I was in the library trying to make sense of my math and chemistry work when Leigh came up to me and sat down. "Need some help?" she asked. I showed her the chapter "Understanding Atomic Structure," which is like this garbled crap on who knows what about things so small but apparently are so important that they are worth making juniors' lives miserable. She told me she was pretty good with that stuff and would help me.

Sure enough, we talked about what was going on for about 15 minutes, and I felt good enough about it to probably pull a *D* on the quiz the next day. We then started talking about cross country and our classes. Before you knew it, the bell rang for lunch to end. During cross country practice, Leigh and I have been running side-by-side some and talking every now and then. She's started sitting next to me in Chemistry. Allen even asked me, "What's up with you and Leigh… are you two talking?"

I guess we are. At first, I couldn't believe she could be interested in me. I know how popular she is around school, and she was on the Homecoming court again this year. I'm more than a little intimidated by girls like that. You know, the popular ones who seem to have everything going for them.

Why would somebody like her want to go out with somebody like me?

But then I remembered that I had sort of made this commitment to myself to just "go for it" when it came to asking girls out. So, when cross country practice was over on Thursday and she had once again run alongside me for most of the afternoon, I just decided to ask her out. I tried not to sound lame, but this was all I could think to say:

"You wanna go do something together this weekend?"

I mean, that's not exactly inviting a girl out for a night of glamour. But she quickly said yes, and asked me what I had in mind. I had just assumed all along that she would say no because she already had dates for both Friday and Saturday. I really had never given any thought that she would actually say yes. So I had no idea where to take her. All I could say was, "What would you like to go do?"

"Whatever you want would be fine with me," she said, and gave me this really big smile.

It's too cold to take her fishing on the river. I really wanted to go deer hunting on Saturday, but I couldn't drag her along on that for our first date. Can you imagine her telling her girlfriends about how cold she got sitting next to me in the woods while waiting for a deer to come by? And how miserable she was the whole time? I thought about asking her if she wanted to go on a picnic up in the mountains, go hiking, then stop somewhere to eat lunch, then hike back. But her mom probably wouldn't be too cool with that idea.

Leigh, I guess, saw that I was confused and started making suggestions. Girls seem to be able to figure out pretty easy when we don't seem to know what we're doing. "I bet you're going deer hunting during the day on Saturday, right?" she asked, and I nodded my head. "Well, why don't you come over to my house after you're finished? We can cook dinner and hang out. Okay?"

I said "Awesome," and that was that. She gave me another big smile and started asking all these questions about what

I liked to eat... what my favorite dessert was and all that kind of stuff. It was like she had been thinking about doing something with me, and already had some ideas. Can you believe that... a girl who's probably been hit on by half the guys in the junior and senior classes?

I've got to admit that I was excited about getting to know her better. I decided to go to my best hunting spot early Saturday morning and try to kill a deer then. The worst possible thing would have been to shoot a deer in the evening and been late for dinner with her. I lucked out and killed a doe on Saturday morning, so I was on time for our 6:00 date.

Leigh had told me that her parents are divorced and she lives with her mom, so that's who came to the door when I knocked. I'm used to parents not particularly being overjoyed when I enter a house, but Leigh's mom was really talkative and said, "My daughter has said a lot of nice things about you." This really put me at ease because I was more than a little bit nervous.

Leigh and I—well, mostly Leigh—cooked grilled salmon with a baked potato and lots of vegetables because she said she was following Coach Guthridge's rules that cross country team members "should eat healthy." We had apple pie for dessert that Leigh had made earlier, and everything tasted great. I mean, the meal was awesome, and her mom just disappeared after I got there.

We then went downstairs and binge-watched *The Office* for two hours and talked the whole time about Pam and Jim and their relationship. She was sitting really close to me the whole time. Finally, I put my arm around her and gave her a kiss. She gave me another one of those huge smiles of hers.

Right before it was time to go, I asked her if she would like to do something next Saturday. She said yes, but I was to plan that date. I told her I could do that. It was a really good day and night.

CHAPTER EIGHTEEN

ELLY

I was glad when Paige came up to me on Thursday at lunch. Paige said that she, Mia, Kylee, and Camila were having a sleepover at her house on Saturday night; and asked if I would like to come. Caleb and I have a date planned for Friday night, but he said he was busy on Saturday, so I told Paige I could come. She said to get there by 6:00 because she was making homemade pizza, and that was exactly when she was going to pop it out of the oven.

On Friday night, Caleb again started complaining about my weight and asked if I had gained some, and I said no. I told him that I had lost almost two pounds this week, and he said it "didn't look that way" to him. I promised I would work on my weight some more this weekend, and that I wanted to please him more than anything. But he just rolled his eyes.

When I got to Paige's house at around 6:15, everybody was already there and eating pizza. Camila told me to sit down and have some. I lied and said I had already eaten a big supper, but the truth was that I hadn't eaten anything since I had a salad for lunch and skipped breakfast. I'll show Caleb that I can look the way he wants me to.

After everybody finished eating, Paige sent Mia, Camila, and Kylee downstairs to pick something to watch on Netflix; and asked me if I would help her clean up the kitchen. As soon as the other girls went downstairs, Paige said, "Is everything okay? Do you want to talk about anything? I've noticed some changes about you."

I told her I felt great, that everything was great in school, and that I had an awesome boyfriend. Paige rolled her eyes and said, "Everybody knows he's out tonight with his other girlfriend. Look, I've seen abusive relationships before. I don't like the way Caleb treats you when you two are together. I don't like the way he cheats on you. I've seen those red marks on your arm on Monday mornings after you've been out with him over the weekend. I can guess where you got them from."

I started to tell her to mind her own business, and that everything was great between Caleb and me. Instead, I started tearing up and couldn't say anything at all.

Paige started talking again. "The reason the other girls and I planned this night was because we're concerned about you."

I stopped crying when she said that, and I said, "So you all have been talking behind my back?! Caleb says he loves me; there's nothing wrong. My parents think he's wonderful."

Paige snapped back, "Parents aren't always right about a guy. Elly, he's no good. We know that. Deep down, you know that, too. You're ruining your health by being so obsessed with your weight and pleasing that jerk. You need help. We want to be there for you."

"This conversation is over," I said, and I went downstairs. Mia, Kylee, and Camila stopped talking as soon as they saw me come down the stairs. I guess they had been talking about me, too.

Mia said, "Is everything alright? You look upset."

Then Kylee added, "You don't look like yourself. You look like you've been sick."

"There's nothing wrong with me!" I screamed. Then I started sobbing so hard, I couldn't stop. Camila came over and held me, and Kylee and Mia were trying to comfort me.

Paige came downstairs and started trying to do the same thing. I must have gone on for like five minutes.

Finally, I stopped crying; and Mia said, "We're just trying to help, Elly. We all think you should break up with Caleb."

"Like you broke up with Luke. That didn't end so well for you, did it?" As soon as I said that, I wished I hadn't. Mia got this really hurt look on her face, and turned her head away from me like she was going to start crying. Everybody knows that Mia's parents forced her to break up with Luke, and that they were perfect for each other. Why did I say that? That's not like me. Caleb has got me all screwed up.

I then blurted out, "I'm sorry, Mia, I didn't mean that. I'm so miserable, I hate myself, and I feel sick all the time inside."

"Girl, that's why you've got to break up with Caleb," said Camila. "You're not going to have any self-respect, and you're not going to feel good about yourself again until you do."

It was then that I finally realized they were all right. I said that when I get back to school on Monday, I would tell Caleb that we were through. But Paige said, "No, do it now. Get it off your mind. He doesn't deserve the courtesy of you breaking up with him in person. Text him right now and say you are done. It'll ruin his date with what's her name, which will make it even better."

So that's exactly what I did. I took out my phone and texted, "I don't like the way you treat me. We're done. Enjoy your date tonight."

After I sent the text, I showed it to everybody; and they all cheered. I felt so much better. I even asked Paige if I could have some of the leftover pizza, and I had three pieces; I was so hungry. The rest of the night, all we did was talk about guys. Kylee had the big reveal. She said she was thinking about breaking up with Marcus, not because he had done anything wrong, but because he was the only boy she had ever dated in high school. She just thought she needed to see what else was out there before she got to college. I need to do the same.

CHAPTER NINETEEN

MARCUS

O n Saturday night, I got a text from Kylee asking if I would like to meet for coffee at around 2:00 Sunday afternoon at the coffee shop. She had this sleepover thing with her friends Saturday night, and I had an away basketball game Friday night, so I figured she just wanted us to have some time this weekend. Normally, we just text and talk on the phone on Sundays; because we've usually gone out on Friday and Saturday nights, or at least hung out somewhere Saturday during the day. Everything has been going really well between us. We almost never argue about anything; and Kylee has told me many, many times that she loves how I've grown and matured as a person since ninth grade. Many times, we've talked about continuing to date when we're at college, like when we come home for a weekend or over the holidays. She wants to go to some small liberal arts college while I want to go to a university, so I know we won't be going to the same school after we graduate.

So, we had just sat down and ordered... I mean, I was just stunned when she said, "We need to talk. I've got something to say." Right away, I was real worried.

Then she continued, "Marcus, you're the only boy I've ever dated in high school. After we broke up in ninth grade, I didn't go out with anybody else for the rest of the year, even though a couple of other guys asked. Then I went out with just you all my sophomore year and all this year, too.

"I want us to take a little break so that we both can go out with other people. We can still go out from time to time, but I don't want us to be exclusive as a couple for a little while. Is that okay? Does that make sense?"

Almost right away, as soon as she started talking, I got suspicious. That "we need to talk" crap is never good. Is there some other guy she wants to date, either at our school or some other school? Can't she see how I've tried to change and be a better man? What gives?

"Marcus, you've got it all wrong," she said. "I'm not even in the talking stage with any other guy. I don't have another guy in mind to replace you. I just need time to work on myself. I have to sort out some stuff. I just want to see what other guys are like before I go away to college. That's all I want, and that's all there is to it. I feel very good about our relationship, but I don't have anything else to compare it with. Do you understand?"

"No, I really don't understand," I said. I wanted to tell her that she had really hurt me by saying all those things. But something deep down wouldn't let me say that she'd hurt me just then. I almost started to tear up; but I didn't want her to see that, either. The longest time went by and there was, like, this awkward silence between us.

I then started thinking about some of the guys in our class who might have been hitting on her or who she seemed overly friendly to. But I really couldn't think of any guy she was really good friends with or might be interested in. Suddenly, I thought maybe one of her friends on Saturday night had put this "take a break from Marcus" crap in her head. It's never good when girls get together for a sleepover and have all night to talk about us guys and our supposed flaws. So I asked her that.

"Marcus, no girl or anybody else or even my parents has put it into my head that we need to take a break from seeing each other exclusively," she said. "You're reading too much into this. I still really, really care for you. It's still possible that one day, we could fall in love and get married. But I won't know you're the one until I go out with other guys and learn more about myself... that's all there is to it. Please believe me."

"Okay," I said. I hurt so bad inside, that was all I could say. I started to blurt out that if she wanted us to take a break, maybe we ought to take a "real break" and not see each other for several months. But I decided not to say that. I didn't want her to feel that I was lashing out at her.

We sat in the coffee shop for another five minutes and didn't say anything to each other. She fiddled with her napkin, coffee cup, and phone; and I took out my phone and answered some texts and looked up some sports scores.

Finally, she said, "Well, I've got to go. I've got some studying to do. You know we've got a big history test this week." She patted me on the back—that's all she did—as she was leaving... not even a goodbye kiss or hug.

After she left, I called my brother and told him everything, every detail that had happened. He said he was so sorry, that maybe she wasn't lying about there not being another guy, that maybe she just did need some space for a while. Joshua said that sometimes girls are like that... there's no predicting them.

I don't know what I'm going to do: whether I'm going to wait for a couple of weeks and ask her out, or start thinking about some other girl who I could date. Right now, I just want the hurt to stop. Guys have feelings, too; but girls never think about that.

CHAPTER TWENTY

MIA

I was really glad when Paige told me she was going to organize a sleepover at her house so that she, Kylee, Camila, and I could talk some sense into Elly about the need for her to break up with that jerk Caleb. It didn't take long for the subject of Elly and Caleb to come up, and we were all trying to get Elly to see that Caleb was no good for her. That's when Elly made a snarky comment to me about why should she take advice from me about breaking up with guys because of the way that Luke and I broke up.

That put-down, I mean, it really hurt me. Elly has never said something like that to me, and I was just dazed that she would talk that way to me. She quickly apologized; but still, the damage was done. I think she knows that I was bothered by what she said. So when everyone else had gone to sleep, she asked if we could go talk.

"I'm really sorry I said that about Luke," she said. "I know I hurt you."

I didn't try to pretend that her remark hadn't hurt. I just nodded my head and said, "It's alright. I know you've been stressed out lately with school and Caleb."

"I have been," she said. "But breaking up with Caleb tonight was really good and healthy for me. Thank you for pushing me. All of you were trying to do the right thing for me."

"You'll find another guy who will be so much better for you," I said. "Somebody new will come into your life before you know it. I bet you can even think of some guys who you'd like to go out with."

Then for the second time that night, Elly stunned me. "I've already had somebody ask me out this fall... Luke," she said.

Elly paused to see what my reaction was. I know I must have had this strange look. Then she quickly went on. "But I turned him down. I mean, I was going with Caleb. And you and Luke used to be a couple. I told Luke no—made it clear that he wasn't to ask me out again.

"I really thought that you and Luke were destined to be together forever. I just thought it would be weird going out with him because of that."

Then I said, "Luke and I are never going to be together again. You should go out with him if he asks you again."

I don't know why I said that to Elly... to be noble and good? I didn't want to be the crazy ex-girlfriend. I don't feel noble and good. Because deep down, from time to time, I fantasize about getting back together with Luke and staying with him forever. I haven't said one word to him all year because of my father's orders. But I really, really feel when we pass in the hall and nod to each other that there's still something between us. All it would take would be one little coincidence of us running into each other somewhere, or just being alone with him for 10 seconds somewhere for all those feelings between us to come back and just burst out. I know... I'm absolutely certain... that's true.

I've heard that he's started going out with Leigh; and there were other girls before her, too. Yes, I've been dating some, too. But it's not the same. Those other girls can't mean anything to him. Then I realized that it had been a long time since either Elly or I had said a word. I came out of my daze, and she was looking at me.

She said, "Well, maybe if Luke asks me out again, I will go out with him. Maybe a sweet, kind boy like Luke is exactly the kind of guy I should go out with. I've never been out with a really nice guy like him before."

"Well, do what you think is best for you," I said. But that's not what I really thought. What I really thought was no, no, no, I don't want Elly to go out with Luke. If she ever went out with him, she'd fall in love with him. I just know it. And he would fall in love with her. I'd never get a second chance with Luke.

"Well, my dad would hate it if I went out with Luke," said Elly. "Of course, he thinks Caleb is perfect, so what does he really know about what kind of guy would be right for me?"

"You're right about your dad not wanting you to be with Luke," I said. "Maybe you should listen to your dad." It sounded so lame when I said that, and I hated myself for being so shallow that I would say something like that. Yes, I would be jealous. I might as well admit it. So now, am I trying to sabotage a hypothetical relationship between Elly and Luke that probably will never happen? Just like Luke and me being together again will probably never happen.

Elly and I kept talking after that; but it must have been close to 2:00 A.M., and I don't remember anything that we said after that time. I was mad at her and mad at myself, and this anger toward my father never goes away. I do nothing but go to school all day and study all night; and I'm stressed out all the time about having money for college, my parents' marriage probably falling apart, not having Luke anymore, and not knowing who I want to be with. Finally, I told Elly, "Let's just go to bed. I'm exhausted." It was probably the only thing I said when we were talking that was the 100-percent truth.

COLLEGE VISITS

CHAPTER TWENTY-ONE

LUKE

A week ago, Ms. Whitney had a meeting for all the juniors who were thinking about going to the local state college so that she could arrange for us to get a tour. All in all, there were about 10 of us. I know everybody who is thinking about going there: Allen, Paige, Mary, Camila, Elly—the same people I have in my classes, pretty much.

Leigh is thinking about going, too. We've been dating for about six weeks now. We've been going out once or twice every weekend. Maybe going out somewhere at night on Friday, then hanging out on Saturday afternoon... going hiking or biking somewhere. When the college visitation thing came up, she asked me if I thought we would be still dating when we went to college. I had never given any thought to how long our relationship might last, so I didn't know what to say at first. Maybe girls are more likely to think about long-range plans than guys? I don't know. So I answered Leigh with something lame like, "What do you think our future will be?"

And she said, "You're the first guy I've ever gone out with who made me feel like I was someone special, who liked me for me." I didn't know what she meant by that, so I asked Allen afterwards. He said that most guys considered Leigh the hottest girl in the school; and pretty much every one of the really popular guys had either hit on her, asked her out, or gone out with her since her freshman year.

She is incredibly beautiful. I mean, that's obvious. I confess I'm a little intimidated by her looks, too… and that she would go out with me, and is even thinking about us as a long-term couple. I do enjoy going out with her, talking about things, having someone to talk to about college and what our futures might be like. But I don't feel the same about her as I used to feel about Mia when we were together—the first time I held her hand, the first time I kissed her.

Or the way I sometimes feel about Elly. When I saw Elly was going on the college visitation trip, my mind just went wild. We're both thinking about being teachers, and we'd probably have some education classes together at college. She's broken up with Caleb, so she's come to her senses about him now. I've thought about asking Elly out again in a month or so when she's had time to get her head on straight once more, and the Christmas holidays are over. But then I'd have to break up with Leigh to do that, and she's done nothing to deserve being treated that way.

The other night, Elly and I had to cover a girls' volleyball game for Yearbook. It was the first time we'd been alone together since I asked her out two months ago. I was a little worried that she would feel awkward around me. She was a little quiet and weird at first. So I thought I should deal with what Ms. Hawk calls "the elephant in the room." You know, the forbidden topic. So I apologized for asking her out when she was dating Caleb, and added that I considered her a really good person and a friend.

That broke the ice, and we ended up having a really good time at the game. She suggested that we go out for coffee afterwards. While we were waiting for our order, I asked to look at the photos she had taken, and started teasing her about all the bloopers and mistakes she had made. She teased me right back by saying, "My photos are the only reason people are going to bother to read your pathetic story. What do you know about girls' volleyball, anyway?" I laughed really hard when she said that.

We then talked about why we wanted to be teachers. We ended up having the same reasons: wanting to help kids, make a difference in their lives, do something important to make a difference in one little corner of the world. I swear, I could have talked all night with her. When she asked whether I wanted to order a second cup of coffee, I was into that. I didn't want the evening to end. Did she feel the same way? Was that why she wanted another cup?

When we had the college visit, I admit that I was more excited to see Elly arrive at the meeting place than when Leigh and her mom did. When the tour guide started talking about where we were going to go during the morning and what the due dates were for such and such forms, I was looking at Elly instead of listening to what was going on.

When we split off into small groups to visit places in the afternoon, I spent most of that time walking around with Leigh and her mom. Later in the afternoon, Leigh heard about a jazz band playing on the campus that night. She asked her mom if she could go to that, and if she and I could meet up with her when the performance was over. I felt honored that Leigh would want to go see the band with me. I mean, I guarantee that those college guys would have been hitting on her all night if she had been there alone.

It was neat, too, to be out at a college listening to music at night with her. I've never experienced anything like that before. The older I've gotten, the more I've realized the few things I've been exposed to. I don't think I ever realized just how poor Mom, Dad, and I were when we were still together. I knew the money thing was bad, but... still. I didn't fully understand how poor we were. Of course, it's not like Granddaddy and I have a lot of nice things in our house, but it's still better than what it was like at Mom and Dad's house. Maybe I should just be thankful for Leigh and get Elly out of my mind.

CHAPTER TWENTY-TWO

ELLY

These college visits on Saturdays are just one more thing in my life to stress out about. Two weekends ago, I visited the local state college; and last weekend, my parents and I drove three hours to the university for one of those guided tours for parents and their "leaders of tomorrow." That was the first corny phrase of the tour guide—where do they find these losers, anyway?

Really, that guy was so annoying with all his stupid, lame jokes, which were usually followed by various sets of parents embarrassing their kids with stupid questions and totally off-the-wall comments. My parents were one of the worst there. Like when my dad asked, "My daughter is really gifted in photography. What kind of photojournalism program do you have here?"

Couldn't he just have asked about the photojournalism program without making an unnecessary comment on my camera skills? Of course, the lame guide said, "Well, we have one of the best programs in the state and country!" But he didn't say why or how it was so wonderful.

Then there was the parent who asked, "Do you provide housing here?" Lady, didn't you even look at the college's website before you got there? I swear. This place of "higher learning" has, like, 20,000 students. Of course, the place has dorms. The tour guide should have said, "No, there's no housing here or anywhere nearby. Your child will have to live in a box under a bridge, sorry. It's a very nice box, though. And our photojournalism offerings are some of the best in the country."

Oh, how about the parents who announced that their darling young man "is a student athlete," and asked what kind of "accommodations" those young men would have? They then announced that they could pay "extra" if "need be" to give their so-athletically-inclined son just the right kind of place to live in. About then, I thought the dad was going to give copies of his financial statements and bank accounts to the assembled multitude.

At least those parents weren't as pathetic as the weird mommy who asked, like, 20 questions about mini-fridges and what the restrictions were on their size. I'll never get those 10 minutes of my life back again.

It was torture spending six hours coming and going with my dad. He just won't let the me-breaking-up-with-Caleb thing die. Dad just kept saying that I "made a huge mistake breaking up with Caleb", and that he "could provide you with the best kind of life—the life you deserve." Well, Pops, maybe I should have shown you the bruises he put on my wrist when he was mad at me, or said some of the choice words he called me when wonderful Caleb was angry at his skinny, little girlfriend who was not allowed to have an opinion of her own.

Mom was almost as bad as Dad was with her comments and unasked-for advice. Mom kept talking about how Caleb's mom said she was so disappointed that I had broken up with her perfect little son, and that Caleb was hoping we could get back together. That little hussy he was dating along with me must have found out what a prize Caleb is, too. I bet two females have dumped him recently.

I've stopped binging and purging since Caleb and I broke up. I realize doing that was stupid and dangerous, and that it could have affected my health long-term. How could I have been so into Caleb that I allowed myself to sink so low just to please his demands that I have the perfect figure— perfect in his eyes, anyway? I've regained three or four pounds since we broke up. I needed to do that. I had gotten too skinny, and I didn't feel good about being so thin. I've got to get a handle on this weight thing. It was just that I was too heavy for so long, then I ended up being too skinny. It's sort of like a metaphor for my whole life. I've always been too much this or too little that. I've never been able to find a happy medium with guys, grades, studying, my self-image, my weight… anything.

I don't want to go to the university, anyway. It's way too big of a school for me, and one of the few things the tour guide did say that was relevant was about the size of the "lecture halls," which could "easily hold 300 or more students." I don't want to be in a class with 300 students. I would just feel lost in a class or a school like that. What if I had a question? What if I didn't understand something? What am I supposed to do then? My parents would be spending all that money for me to go there, and most of the professors wouldn't even know my name.

I think the thing for me to do is go to the local college. I could still live in a dorm and get to know people from out of state and around the country. Then, if I didn't like dorm life, it would be no big deal to live at home and commute in my sophomore year.

I haven't started dating anybody in the three weeks Caleb and I have been broken up. A couple of guys have been hitting on me and texting dumb stuff. But I don't know, I'm just not ready to start another relationship right now. I've got to get my own head back on straight. The nicest time I've had with a boy recently was when Luke and I went to cover a girls' volleyball game. He had me laughing at everything he said, but the sweetest thing he did was apologizing for asking me out months ago when I was going out with Caleb. Can you imagine how Dad would act if I announced I was going out with the orphan son of a lowlife father? I'll find a new boyfriend eventually, and this next guy will treat me better.

CHAPTER TWENTY-THREE

MARCUS

Two weeks ago, my parents took me to the state university to look it over. We went on one of those tours that you can sign up for where some upperclassman takes people around, and you're supposed "to see everything." But all we saw were the outsides of stone buildings where such and such classes were held, and the outsides of dorms where you might live. What good is all that, anyway? The tour guide was some doofus who kept saying lame crap like "This school is rated high in student happiness" and "Our city has a low crime rate." I mean, would he have told us that everybody who comes there is miserable, and we'd better not leave the university grounds unless we want to get mugged? Get real.

The other day, in seventh-period Art I class, I heard Allen and Paige talking about getting a group together to drive to the university and make a tour without parents and tour guides. I said I wanted in on that. Then Mia must have overheard them, and said she would like to go if it was okay… that her parents had been talking about taking her there, but never seemed to have the time. Paige said that she could drive us up there, and everybody could chip in with the gas. We could go in the morning, get there around noon, and look things over. Then we could go into the city at night and see what was happening. I was down with all that.

I told Dad and Mom about wanting to go to the university with friends, and they both were good with it. But later that evening, Dad came up to my room. He looked so serious when he came in that I automatically thought I had screwed up somehow about something. But no, he said he had come to give me "The Talk."

"Marcus," he started. "Your mom and I really appreciate the maturity you've shown the last six months or so. I think we made a mistake in giving you too much too soon because we could afford to. Maybe that caused you not to grow up as soon as you would have if you'd had to struggle for things. But that's our fault, not yours.

"I think you're finally appreciating the struggles that your grandparents made. We live in a really nice house in a really nice neighborhood because of the sacrifices my parents and your mom and me made.

"But you've lived in an ideal world your whole life. Before you go off on your college visit, you really need to be super-aware that there are still places in this country where all our respectability won't mean a thing if some policeman who has personal issues about blacks pulls you over. When that happens, you've got to know how to react so that you are not in danger."

I said, "*If* that happens, I..." but Dad immediately interrupted me.

"Marcus, not if, when," he said. "It happened to me when I was about your age. Back in 1986, I was driving a brand-new green Honda Acura that my parents had just given me. I was pretty excited, and had turned the radio up real loud. I was driving through this upper-class white neighborhood on the way to our home when the next thing I knew, a police car pulled me over.

"While I was sitting in the car talking to the officer, two more cars pulled up; and out came cops and a drug-sniffing dog. Son, I was raging inside and crying outside. I was basically guilty of driving while black. Because I was in a nice car and playing loud music, they assumed I had to be a drug dealer.

"But my dad had given me 'the talk,' and I had enough sense to just say 'yes, sir' and 'no, sir' and keep my head down when they questioned me. They let me call Dad, and he came down and did the 'humble black man' thing; and they let me go. So don't think something like this couldn't happen to you. You understand me?"

I stood there. I've kept what he said in mind.

On the way up to the college, at first, I felt a little awkward sitting in the back seat with Mia while Allen and Paige were in the front. They've been dating since they were freshmen... they're even talking about going to the same college. Mia is super-hot and smart, but I always got the impression when we were freshmen that she couldn't stand me. I can understand that; I was a real jerk then. She's been friendlier since ninth grade.

When the trip was planned, I called the basketball coach's office and asked if I could possibly meet with somebody about maybe being a walk-on if I went there. The secretary seemed indifferent to me. I can understand that. Who knows how many phone calls like that she gets every day? When I was a ninth-grader, I was absolutely sure I was going to play pro football and basketball after college. Now, I've been reduced to practically begging to be a non-scholarship walk-on for a small-time Division 1 school.

I've been averaging 13 points per game as a small forward this year; but since my leg injury, I don't have that old explosiveness. I know that's why Coach Henson moved me to small forward. I'm still a starter, and I know I'll start next year as a senior, but no D-1 school is going to want an undersized small forward who's a step or two slow and doesn't average 20 points a game.

So, I was a little surprised—and really happy—when Assistant Coach Ford called me that same night. He said the coaching staff knew who I was, and had actually had their eye on me. Then came the downer. The guy asked how my leg was feeling, and if I "got that great vertical leap back." I said the leg was coming along, and I'd be back to normal by next year.

I don't really believe that. I fear I'm never going to be back to what I was. Then the assistant coach said he'd be glad to meet with me, and he'd arrange for me to get two comp tickets for the game Saturday night. Plus, he set up an appointment to talk with him at 3:00 that afternoon. Man, I was floored at all that. Maybe I could walk-on; then if I did alright, I could get a scholarship later.

We got to the university around noon; then walked around for a couple of hours, stopping and talking to the students we ran into, visited the library and bookstore, walked through some classroom buildings... that type of stuff. The most beneficial thing was talking to the students. Most of them seemed pretty happy to be there.

Of course, I went to see Assistant Coach Ford by myself. He seemed like an okay dude, and we talked for about 15 minutes. Then he asked me if he could be blunt, and I said yeah.

"Marcus," he said, "We would definitely like for you to try to walk-on if you come here. The competition will be stiff because a lot of guys want to walk-on. But if your leg gets back to what it was, you could be that diamond in the rough. At the very least, you could be a student manager, and see how a D-1 school goes about its business. If you ever wanted to coach, say, high school basketball, we could give you a good reference."

At first, I felt real low because I'd been reduced to probably being a towel boy. But I've got to suck it up and take what I can get, I guess. The assistant coach and I agreed to stay in touch, and that the team would "keep you on our radar."

That night, while the four of us were eating dinner, Allen and Paige said that they wanted to go into town and see a band that was playing. It would cost about $30 for them to go, but it would be worth it. Mia seemed hesitant to go, so I told her about the two free tickets to the game and asked if she wanted to come with me. She said yes, but I think the only reason she did was because her family doesn't have any money. It was kind of neat going to the game with her and explaining what was going on. She's a pretty interesting girl.

CHAPTER TWENTY-FOUR

MIA

I finally had a chance to make my first college visit. It was to the state university; I went with Allen, Paige, and Marcus. However, I'd really like to go somewhere that has more of a medical-school reputation than this college does. I feel certain I can get a scholarship, maybe even a major one, somewhere. My parents keep saying that they are going to take me on a college visit, but they argue so much these days; and the money situation seems worse than it ever has been now that my father is only working part-time. I don't think the two of them could stand to be in the same car together, let alone if we have enough money to drive to an out-of-state university.

I'm not helping to bring in any money because there's no time for me to babysit or work somewhere part-time with all the tough classes I'm taking. I'm so stressed over my parents' problems and school that it seems all I do is worry and study.

At first, I was really excited to be going on the college visit. Paige is one of my best friends, along with Elly and Camila. Even Marcus is a pretty good guy; he has grown up a lot since he was a freshman. Of course, he was so immature, he had nowhere to go but up.

For the trip, I packed my lunch and dinner. I only had $10.00 in my purse, so I thought I would be fine with the expenses. But when we met up, Paige said she would need

$10.00 from each of us for the gas expense. Then Allen and Marcus talked about where we would be eating out for lunch, and both of the guys said there was a really nice restaurant near the college that we could check out for dinner. Plus, we all needed to discuss where we would be going that night for entertainment.

I was able to bluff my way through the lunch stop by saying that I had brought a sandwich. But I was so hungry that I ate both my lunch and dinner sandwiches, and then I had to worry all afternoon what I was going to do when we went out for dinner. I remember when Luke and I were dating last year, after his mom had died and his dad was drunk all the time, how he never had enough money or food. And now, with my parents' situation and the financial issues, I'm feeling the same stress. I don't have anyone to lean on like he had me. I still miss him, and none of the guys I've dated this year have even been close to Luke.

With Allen and Paige being a couple, it was a little awkward for Marcus and me to sort of have to pair up for the trip. They had places at the college they wanted to visit together, so Marcus and I ended up going just about everywhere with each other. He's going to be a history major, so he wanted to visit some guys who he had found out were history majors. And of course, he had to go by the basketball team's office and talk to people there, so I went with him for those things except I hung out at the bookstore when he was with the coach. When he said he had two free tickets to the game that night and asked if I wanted to go with him, I said yes. Not because I particularly wanted to go to the game or be with him, but because I didn't have any money to go with Allen and Paige out to the dinner-theater date that they had planned. Me paying for a dinner and a play was out of the question.

With all my studying, I hadn't even had time to plan for the trip or decide what I wanted to see. So I asked Marcus if it would be alright if we visited the medical library and where some of the classes are held. I talked to some of the students at the library, and they seemed happy enough to be there. I really didn't get much out of the talks or the visits to the medicine-related things. The whole time I was going around, I kept worrying that I should be home in my room studying.

At least that kept me from worrying about not having any money for dinner. When it was time for Marcus and me to go eat, I finally had to confess that I didn't have enough money to go out, which was embarrassing. He said that his parents had given him enough money to eat out and to go somewhere later. Since the game was going to be free, he had enough money for my dinner, too; and that I could pay him back. It was nice of him to put things that way; it made me feel less embarrassed.

Dinner with him was actually really nice. I didn't know that he had an *A* average in so many classes, and that he wants to be a historian of some sort. I was surprised that he really wanted to know about my decision to be a pediatrician. I was also impressed that he realized that his football-playing days were over, and that he would probably never be the basketball player he once was because of the torn ACL he had last year.

When we were at the game, I had a good time, too. Marcus kept up a running commentary on what was going on between the two teams, and what their respective strengths and weaknesses were. I was so impressed that I said, "Have you ever thought about going into coaching on either the high school or college level?"

"Actually, I have," he said. "Maybe that's how I could get my basketball fix." After the game, we had to walk about 30 minutes to meet Allen and Paige; and we talked the whole time. It's the first time in a long time that I've actually enjoyed doing anything at all.

CHRISTMAS BREAK

CHAPTER TWENTY-FIVE

LUKE

I decided about two weeks before Christmas break that I'd better try to get a part-time job during the holidays. You know, employers are just standing in line waiting for 17-year-olds to come by their personnel office. Granddaddy's on a fixed income, and he's been really good about giving me money when I needed it. But I've felt guilty about it the whole time. He's right, though, about me concentrating on academics and running cross country this semester. That's probably more important in the long run for me getting into a college.

I didn't actually do too bad in cross country. I finished fifth in the regional 5,000 meters—not too shabby for my first year running, so I should do even better next year. Maybe if I have a good season, some school will give me a break financially if I run cross country in college.

I did find a temporary job; it was for eight hours a day during the holidays at a local combination lawn care, nursery, and Christmas tree lot that needed help. I would be in charge of selling Christmas trees from 9 to 5 until Christmas Eve, then do fill-in jobs for employees who were taking time off for the holidays to be with their families.

Actually, the selling trees thing wasn't too bad. Of course, some of the customers were real jerks. Some guy would come in with his two or three kids and the man would complain about such and such a tree "not being full enough" and another guy would whine about some tree costing too much and try to bargain the price down. As if I had the power to restore a tree's "fullness" or make an executive decision on the price of an evergreen.

A couple of guys who dropped out of my high school were working there. I barely knew them because one of them was a year older than me, and the other was two years older. But they nodded at me in recognition on my first day there. One of them, John, said, "Did you drop out, too?"

I said, "No, just working here during the break."

"Yeah, that's what I thought, too," he said. "I just thought I'd work here during summer break between junior and senior year. But I hated school so much, I never did go back when school started up again."

John went on to say that he was thinking about taking some night classes for his GED and get some tech training, too. He said he was "going to do it, real soon."

Maybe he will, too; I hope he will, for his sake. Still, I've often heard guys talk about going back to school after dropping out, but never seen or heard of many doing it. I know I was headed for dropping out until Mia came into my life and changed my whole attitude about everything. I think Mia's persuasion and Dad telling me to drop out made the difference in my staying in school. Him telling me what to do made me want to do the opposite. I don't miss him at all, and I rarely think about him anymore unless it's in a bad way... like right now.

I didn't see Leigh but two times over the break. We've been dating a little less than three months, I guess. So, we had that awkward talk about whether we should get each other something for Christmas. That "giving of gifts to girls for Christmas" thing is just a minefield. How long do you have to date a girl before you buy her a Christmas present? What kind of gift should it be? How much should you spend? Should the gift be something sexy, pretty, or practical? Who knows what? And what happens if the girl gives a guy something and then they break up a few days later? Is the guy supposed to get his gift back? There ought to be a rule book for this. I sure as heck don't know what to do.

Leigh and I went around and around about the gift. The one thing I didn't want to do was hurt her feelings. We finally decided that her Christmas present to me would be for her to cook us dinner one night at her and her mom's house. And mine to her would be to prepare a picnic lunch for us the Sunday after Christmas and go on a hike. I think that took the pressure off both of us.

I do like her. I do enjoy her company. She's pretty interesting to be with; and obviously, she's gorgeous. Yeah, looks are important, but I know enough now about dating that appearance isn't the main thing. More than anything else, I want a girl who will fuss at me when I do something stupid, praise me when I do something wonderful, and be a real partner in life. I want her to have a good heart. I want us to have kids one day and be absolutely sure that she would be a great wife and mom.

Leigh has lots of good qualities. But I don't see her as someone I will be with a year from now, or even by the end of the school year. I hope she doesn't want us to go to prom. She's always been on the prom court, and she will definitely be on it this year, too. I would hate going to that; and I couldn't afford to go, anyway. Deep down, I worry that she likes me better than I like her. I don't know how to express this. I don't feel magic when I'm around her. Is that even the right word?

CHAPTER TWENTY-SIX

ELLY

Mom, Dad, and my brothers were all psyched up about going to the beach for four days over Christmas; but I didn't want to go with them. I didn't want to stay at home, either, with no boyfriend to keep me company. Somebody like Mary would have called me. We would have probably gone out and done something stupid. I've done enough stupid things in high school already from dating the wrong kinds of boys like Caleb to listening to people like Mary. I might as well face it—and admit it—that most of my problems in high school have been caused by my own immaturity.

Maybe it shows that I'm growing up a little because I realized I've been immature. On the other hand, if I really were a mature person, I wouldn't be worried about staying at home by myself and inevitably doing something really stupid once some sort of temptation came along. Mom and I were going around and around on one of our never-ending arguments, with her saying, "Why can't you go to the beach with the rest of us?" to "I don't want you to spend the holidays at home by yourself." I don't think she trusts me to be alone in the house. Really, why should she trust me when I don't trust myself?

I think one of the reasons why I didn't want to go to the beach was because it would have dredged up old memories of last summer, when Caleb and I were there. Or I would have had to listen all during the five-hour drive about "How nice it was last summer when you and Caleb were together." And "Oh, by the way, are you two making any progress about patching things up?"

Finally, Mom came up with a great idea. "Why don't we drop you off at Aunt Jenny's house on our way down to the beach?" I went for that immediately. Aunt Jenny is Mom's older sister, and she has always been my favorite aunt. Ever since I was a little kid, we've always been able to talk. I've always trusted her not to go blabbing things to Mom.

After my parents dropped me off, Aunt Jenny fixed us a nice lunch of broiled chicken and baked asparagus in olive oil, just the kind of healthy meal I should eat more of instead of what I've been eating. I'm still a few pounds underweight, and definitely too thin after my binge-purging episodes as "Caleb's perfect-looking girlfriend." Of course, Aunt Jenny noticed how I looked right off, and asked me about it after lunch.

"I was in a bad relationship," I said. "He kept hammering at me to lose more weight, and look and dress a certain way. So I started to binge-purge, and I'm only now getting my life back together."

"It's okay, sweetie," she said. "We all do dumb things one time or another because of guys. Now, let's talk about your future. Do you still want to be an elementary school teacher? Have you made your college choice? Have you finally figured out what kind of boy you do want?"

It was so good and natural being with Aunt Jenny; and I really opened up to her, unlike Mom, who just doesn't seem to want to listen to me and is so judgmental if I don't see things her way. I told Aunt Jenny that I was definitely going to be a teacher, and that I thought the small local college would be a good fit for me. Also, I didn't have any boys in my life right now. It was too soon after Caleb, still.

"That's not what I asked you about boys," she said. "I

asked you if you knew what kind of boy you should be looking for. Have you settled on that yet?

She really made me think when she said that. "The kind of boy I want," I said, "is one who will make me feel safe and secure. Who will treat me with respect and be my life partner and be a good father to our children. But I also want romantic love, deep down being in crazy love, 'stars in my eyes' love with a guy. Is that too much to ask? I'm beginning to think that it is."

"No, it's not too much to ask," she said. "Don't ever settle, Elly, for a guy who isn't everything you want. That's what leads to bad marriages... when one member, or both members, of the couple settles. Do you know a guy who would be perfect for you?"

"Luke," I blurted out. At first, I was sorry when I said that, but then I wasn't. His name must have been in my head, just rattling around in my subconscious. "But I've already rejected him once this year, and now he has a girlfriend. Mom and Dad, especially Dad, would hate it if we started dating, and if I fell in love with him."

"Well, your mom and dad aren't the ones who will be spending their lives with this Luke or whatever guy you do truly fall for; you will... think about that long and hard. Besides, I'm your mom's older sister. I'll tell her what's what if you decide to go after this Luke boy. Think about what you want and go for it. Follow your heart, sweetie. If you don't, you'll always have regrets about the boy who got away."

I will think about it, but not quite yet. I want to get healthy and my head on straight before I start dating again. I told Aunt Jenny that, and she agreed. We had a great time together.

CHAPTER TWENTY-SEVEN

MARCUS

Over the years, I've spent a bunch of Christmas breaks at swanky places because my family is well-off. This Christmas, Mom and Dad said they wanted to take me, Joshua, and his girlfriend, Jordan, to Washington, D.C. and tour the sights. But I said I'd just as soon stay home. I would've liked to have spent some time with my brother since he would be on break from college, too. But we wouldn't have gotten too much face time if we were all in a vehicle together and traveling or going to visit something all the time. I was glad that Mom and Dad trusted me to be alone over the break. They know I'm not the little jerk I was when I was a ninth-grader.

Another reason I wanted to stay at home was because Mia asked me to come over to dinner at her house one night as a way of repaying me for buying her dinner that night when we visited the college. Us eating dinner together at college wasn't a date, not even close; and it wasn't a date when I came over to her house. I understand that her family doesn't have any money; and she couldn't afford to take me out somewhere as repayment or pay me money, either. I bought her dinner because she didn't have any money. I wasn't trying to get in good with her or anything.

Still, she's an impressive girl. I mean, she's the smartest

person in our class, and maybe the whole school. She's really beautiful in an "I don't care what you think about my appearance way." I can understand why Luke was so into her our freshman and sophomore years.

It was a little weird at her house. Her mom met me at the door, and I saw her dad sitting in an armchair. The guy didn't acknowledge me being there, or talk to his wife or Mia the whole time. He just sat there in like this stony silence. Something's not right about that house... about that man.

Mia seemed glad to see me, and she thanked me over and over again for the dinner out. She served this great-tasting Mexican entrée, chicken tinga tostaditas. I told her the dish was amazing, and said I'd never tasted chicken quite like that. She laughed and said, "That's because that chicken was walking around in our backyard until about three hours ago."

I mean, she actually killed a chicken to feed us. I started to ask her how to kill a chicken, but I figured that was probably not the kind of thing to talk about over dinner. For dessert, we had strawberry cheesecake chimichanga—another Mexican dish that I'd never had before that was really good.

After dinner, Mia said we needed to get out of the house before "the nightly fighting begins," and asked if I wanted to take a walk. I'd never been on this side of town before. The houses were so much smaller than the ones in my neighborhood, and most of the people I saw were Hispanic. But there were some poor white and black families there, too. I wouldn't want to live in a neighborhood like that. The walk, the visit, the whole thing made me realize how good I've had it my entire life—a black kid who's lived in an upper-class neighborhood with parents who are ultra-successful with their jobs and in a successful marriage. No wonder my parents were all over me about my attitude and immaturity when I was a kid.

Mia and I hadn't been walking long when she said, "My father... my mama, I apologize. I think they're about ready to separate. Mama has sort of hinted to me about a trial separation coming soon. She keeps saying, 'Don't tell your younger sisters.' But they know. How could they not know with all the yelling and fighting going on all the time?"

"How are you holding up?" I asked.

"I'll be glad when he's gone," she said. "He broke Luke and me up..." She got quiet for a while. "I'm sorry. I shouldn't have gotten into my personal life."

"That's okay, that's okay," I said. "It's a small junior class. Everybody knows the business of everybody else. Luke's a good dude. I've worked with him on some projects this year in history."

There was more silence for a while after I said that, and I thought maybe I shouldn't have kept talking about Luke. Then I thought I'd better change the subject. So I said, "Do you think you might go to the state university?"

"Yes, I do," she said. "A couple of days ago, they offered me a full scholarship based on need and my academic success. The college has a really good pre-med program, which would be perfect. It's close to home, but not too close... you know what I mean. So, yes, I accepted the offer. I may even go up there this summer to live and take classes. Maybe I could graduate in three years if I kept doing that. And, well, it would get me away from all the drama at my house."

She then asked about me and whether I might go there. I told her it was a real possibility. Then I started thinking, if we both went there... would I want to ask her out? Heck, would I want to ask her out this year? But I thought that in the past, I've gotten into girl trouble by not taking things slow. Right now, I think I'd better settle for the guy Mia wants to talk to when she wants a male perspective.

So I said, "If you ever want to talk to someone about, you know, the parent problems or going to college, or whatever, call or text me. Here's my number."

"Thank you, I will," she said and smiled.

It was a pretty interesting evening.

CHAPTER TWENTY-EIGHT

MIA

L ife is strange, and it sucks, too... sometimes in the same day and night. One day over Christmas, I had two guys act semi-interested in me—guys who I sort of might be interested in a little... maybe. Mateo is this guy I met in my college Human Anatomy and Physiology I class first semester, and will be in the Part II class this coming semester. One morning, he texted me about the research paper that we'd been assigned. I answered, then we texted back and forth for the next half-hour about the topics. Finally, he called and asked if I would be interested in him coming over to pick me up and going to the college library to do research. He knows I don't have a car.

I said sure. We ended up getting there around 10; and worked for about three hours on the college's computers, missing lunch. I really need to have a laptop, but we can't afford one; and it's so frustrating at home that the five of us have to share two PCs. Isabella and Emma are eight and 10 years old now, so they don't have much homework. But our father is on one computer for what seems like hours on some nights, and he won't get off when we ask him to. So, my sisters and I end up fighting over that other computer just about every night.

Anyway, Mateo said because I had helped him out on

his paper, he would buy me coffee and a sweet roll at the college snack shop, so I said okay. I was really hungry and like always, I didn't have much money on me. I'm sick of that. I'm studying for a job that will pay me really well one day, but I'm counting pennies constantly to get ready for that job.

Mateo and I ended up talking for about an hour. Finally, he said, "Would your boyfriend mind us having had lunch together?" I know he really just wanted to know if I have a boyfriend. He was sort of fishing around and trying to work up his courage to ask me out. Boys are so transparent. I get tired of "playing dumb" around them, like I don't understand what they mean when they say something.

Finally, I decided to just be coy about his remark. I said, "Well, some of my boyfriends might mind, and some of them probably wouldn't. You want me to take a quick survey of all seven of them?"

He laughed at that. Then I told him I had to get home and do some chores, which I really did have to do because I had to kill one of our old hens that had stopped laying eggs. Marcus was coming over for dinner (that chicken was going to be our dinner entrée) as a way of me paying him back for taking me out to eat when we visited the state university— once again, because I didn't have enough money to pay for my own meal. But one other reason why I wanted to go then was so that Mateo wouldn't have time to ask me out, if that was what he was working up his courage to do. I didn't know whether I would have said yes or no. I just didn't want to have to agonize over one more thing right now. School and my whole messed-up family situation is enough stress.

Marcus seemed interested in me that night, too. Now, my father would probably like it if I went out with Mateo because he's Hispanic. And daddy dearest might even like me going out with Marcus even though he's black, just because his family is rich. Frankly, I don't care what my father likes or wants. Isabella and Emma keep asking me, "What's the matter with Poppa? Why are him and Mama fighting all the time?"

And I keep telling them nothing's the matter, which is a lie. I hate myself for lying to them, but what am I supposed to do? Tell the truth? Say "Our father is only working two or three days a week at his construction job, and doesn't seem too concerned about it. That's why our parents are fighting. Get over it!" Or how about this lie: "Mama and Poppa aren't really arguing all the time. That's just their way of teasing each other. Don't worry, little sisters."

Maybe Marcus came over just because he didn't want me to feel embarrassed about paying for our dinner that night. Maybe he's not really interested in me. But I think he might be. Mary said something one time in English Honors this year: that guys and girls can't really be friends with each other; that deep down in a guy's head, when he is being friendly, he's thinking what it would be like to be with that girl.

I don't like Mary; she's boy-crazy and is always chasing after guys and acting desperate. But I think she's nailed male behavior—they can't be real friends with us. And I'm not sure we can be real friends with them without thinking about the possibilities of dating them. Like what I'm doing right now with one guy who asked me to study with him and another guy who went on a college visit with me.

I've got to go study and get all this stuff out of my head. My parents and their screwed-up relationship are something I have zero control over. But I can help my sisters get through this mess, and I can help myself have a better future. I can have at least some control over those things.

THE MINOR
CHARACTERS

CHAPTER TWENTY-NINE

LEIGH

Ever since seventh grade, I've had boys constantly hitting on me. Back then, it was just them doing stupid stuff: tripping me when I was walking down the hall; telling me their dumb jokes; constantly asking me to dance with them during those awful, awkward middle school parties. Come to think of it, the boys didn't improve much with their flirting when I got to high school. About the only thing different was that by then, they were telling me how hot and beautiful I was.

Other girls think that a really pretty girl has it easy—that it must be so wonderful being so popular with the guys. I've known I was really pretty since like forever; and let me tell you, it's not as wonderful as it seems. Mom started letting me wear makeup when I was in eighth grade, which was when I went out on my first real date. By tenth grade, I was spending a good hour every morning putting just the right number of curls in my long blonde hair and making sure my eyes and the blush on my cheeks were absolutely perfect. I was obsessed with how I looked. I didn't care about my grades even though I was taking only honors subjects. Just give me a *C*, teacher, and pass me on to the next year... where there would be more guys to conquer and more guys falling all over themselves trying to get me to like them.

I had to be perfect in appearance; I had to be the perfect

cheerleader. I had my pick of all the hottest guys in school. I was either dating guys a couple of years older than me who were big-time athletes like Paul and Richard, or were really sexy, or had a lot of girls after them like Caleb and Matthew. And all it got me was heartache and a reputation for being an airhead—and worse—the rumors that I was sleeping with every guy I went out with.

I don't know who started those rumors, probably little harpies like Mary or guys I dumped like Caleb and Matthew. Both of those jerks were absolutely the worst human beings I've ever been around. Why on earth was I ever into them? They were just eye candy for females—shallow, stuck-up, disgusting little boys in men's bodies. But they were the type of boys I wanted to have by my side then.

The whole summer between tenth and eleventh grade, I was super-depressed. I barely hung out with my friends at all, and I didn't go on any dates all summer. Believe me, it was a pleasure turning down some of those guys who called; and I enjoyed not answering texts from some of those losers. Right before it was time to go back to school, I finally decided on how I was going to change things.

I decided that I was through with getting up early to put on makeup… and that I wasn't going to wear any makeup to school at all. I was going to put my hair up in a bun or a ponytail, and leave it at that. I wasn't going to wear short skirts or dresses to school anymore, just jeans. I was going to quit the cheerleading squad. I loved the girls on that squad, I loved our coach, I loved that we were real athletes, and we had to be in great physical shape to do what we did. But I was tired of dressing up in those outfits.

And most importantly, I was going to make the A-B honor roll and try out for cross country instead of cheering. I was going to do something more constructive with my life than caring about boys.

And wouldn't you know it, as soon as I had sworn off guys forever—or at least, during eleventh grade—along came Luke. A guy who I don't think I had even said one word to in our freshman and sophomore years—a guy who, if I had ever thought about at all, I would have considered a dork.

That day during cross country practice when I hurt my leg, he was so kind and respectful to me. He asked me for permission to touch my leg to see how badly it was hurt. Can you believe that? Most guys would have been making smart remarks and hitting on me when I was sitting there in agony on the trail. Not Luke, though.

We slowly started to run together during practice, we started talking, and then we found out we had things in common. We both have had messed-up home lives, with my dad deserting Mom and me when I was in seventh grade. You know, the classic "other woman" scenario. And both of Luke's parents died when he was in tenth grade. Like me, his grades have never been the best, and we are both trying to change that. I'm almost as bad in math as he is. Math kept us both off the honor roll in the first semester. Well, math did for me; math and chemistry kept Luke off. He and his granddaddy don't have much money and don't live in a nice house, just like Mom and me. So, yeah, Luke and I have a lot in common. He just won me over by not trying to win me over—like every other guy I've ever been involved with. Does that make sense?

I wanted Luke to ask me out so bad, and he still hadn't. I couldn't stand it. I tried to flirt with him, but not in an obvious way, if you know what I mean. When he finally did ask me out, I felt like a ninth-grader going out on her first date. We've been dating for three months now, and I don't want to go out with anybody else. Most of the time, all I do is cook him dinner at my house, or we will go hiking or driving somewhere and have a picnic. We've only been out to dinner twice; and both times, we split the check. I insisted because he doesn't have any more money than my mom and I do. I asked him if he wanted us to be exclusive, and he said no… that he wanted me to be free to go out with other guys if I wanted to.

At first, I thought that was kind of sweet. But then I started to worry that he's not into me as much as I'm into him. That's the first time I've ever worried about something like that. He's a special guy.

CHAPTER THIRTY

CALEB

I'm pissed off about everything right now. Ms. Roche gave me a *D* on my English 11 A.P. research paper for the nine weeks, which caused me to have a *D* for the semester. She claimed that my paper on *The Crucible* "lacked analysis," and she couldn't see my "voice." Well, of course, my *voice* wasn't in the paper. Ashley, my girlfriend who goes to Wilson, is a sophomore and wrote most of the paper. She's an airhead and will do anything I tell her to do. She said she read the Wikipedia summary of it. That should have been good enough for a *C*, anyway.

It was bad enough that I read part of that crap book without Roche getting all up in my face about what was wrong about the paper. I don't have time to waste part of my life on dumb Puritans who lived in the 1500s or whatever century they were in. What's really important to know is that Ms. Roche has such a sad life that she had time to complain about my *voice*. How pathetic is that!?

I told Mom that she had to call Roche to set her straight and change my grade. It was a real pleasure hearing Mom give Roche what was coming to her over the phone. I was really pissed when Mom said Roche wouldn't change the grade. So Mom called Mr. Caldwell next and told him how incompetent Roche was, and how Caldwell should talk to her about how unfair she was to certain students. Caldwell stuck up for Roche, can you believe that? I swear this school has completely fallen apart this year.

I got a *C* or a *D* on every single subject in the first semester, except for an *F* in Chemistry. This school is filled with teachers who don't know how to teach. Dad said he'd pay for me to go to the local private school if I wanted. But I don't want to. I know some of the girls who go there, and they're all ugly bitches. Dad's still mad at Coach Dell for taking away my starting quarterback job. Dad said the teachers are as incompetent as the sports coaches at the school—he's right.

Matthew came over on Friday night, and we tossed back grape Smirnoff malts until we were so blind that we couldn't stay awake. Matthew is between girlfriends right now, and I'm ticked off at Ashley right now because of the paper. So, we've been hanging out more than we usually do. He knows what a dumb bitch Elly can be because he dated her sophomore year. I prefer to be dating two or three chicks at once; but Elly dumped me last month, and Elise's dad made her break up with me. I can have any girl at school I want, and it's always good to have another girl or two on the side from different schools. I know plenty of other girls from other schools who go to our church. It's just a matter of time before I have a ton of babes under my spell again. Right now, it just feels good to kick back on weekends with bros like Matthew.

The other day, we really put one over on Roche. Matthew said he had a sore throat and had to go to the nurse. A few minutes later, I told her that I had to go to the bathroom. At first, she said no because "one person is already out of the room," but then I told her that I was holding back farts and really had to go. Saying that always works. No teacher wants to be in the room with a fart factory.

Matthew and I met up in the bathroom and threw back a couple of vodka and oranges… I felt a whole lot better about reading *The Great Gatsby* when we got back. The buzz hit me during Martin's A.P. History class. There's nothing like a good morning nap when you're studying World War I. I mean, who wants to hear about trench warfare and people with the flu puking their guts out in holes? What's that got to do with my life or anything that is happening today? I'll answer that... nothing, that's what.

I'm thinking about getting back together with Elly. I've had Mom call Elly's mother several times to tell her how sorry I am that I "upset" her daughter. Mom also said, and I didn't have to tell her to say it, that Elly was her "favorite out of all the girls that Caleb has dated." I can manipulate Mom into doing just about anything I want her to; but this time, I didn't even have to. Women are like putty in my hands. I've got the gift.

I'm going to wait another couple of weeks before I make a move on Elly. I've noticed that she's not dating anybody right now. She probably regrets dumping me. She's really hot since she lost all that weight. She wasn't worth my time before that happened. Back in our freshman and sophomore years, I could tell that she was really into me. But she was just another fat chick with stupid-looking glasses and messed-up hair then.

I don't know where I'm going to college. Since I quit the football team, I'm not going to get a sports scholarship, that's for sure. Maybe I could go to the state university and try out as a walk-on. I'd probably blow away all those scholarship quarterback jocks. But would the coaches have enough sense to give me the starting QB job? Or would they feel that they messed up so bad by not giving me a scholarship that it would make them look bad if I were the best man for the job? I could see the coaches, if they're anything like the loser high school coaches I've been around, copping out like that. I could really go for those college cheerleaders. That's reason enough for me to try to walk-on.

CHAPTER THIRTY-ONE
MS. HAWK

This is my third year of teaching. I'll get tenure after this year, and all my evaluations by Mr. Caldwell have been great. Yet, on too many days, I have these horrible doubts that I'm not a good teacher, that I'm not getting through to the hard-to-reach kids… and that I have no idea what I'm doing.

The workload is just crushing sometimes. I go home with papers to grade that take up hours; and I wake up sometimes in the middle of the night worrying about some kid, or that I forgot to bring up some important point in class. Then I get up *early* the next day and go to school *early* so that I'll be super-prepared, and some crisis always seems to come up. I have to go to faculty meetings, English department meetings, special ed meetings, meetings with parents, meetings with administrators for evaluations… meetings, meetings, meetings. Every one of them adds up to me not being able to get my grading and planning done, which then leads to me taking more and more work home.

I've got no boyfriend, and no love life whatsoever. I'm 25, and my friends from college all have steady guys or are engaged or married. Plus, they're all making 10 to 20 thousand dollars more than me and only working eight-hour days. I'm still paying off my college loans, living in a cheap apartment, and driving a 12-year-old piece of junk. Did I mention that I spent last Saturday morning at a car repair shop? Maybe I should buy a newer used car, but the higher car payments would likely mean that I'd even have a harder time making ends meet.

One of the History teachers, Mr. Martin, has asked me out twice. He seems nice enough, but I've turned him down both times. I said I was overwhelmed with school work, which is true; but I could have used a dinner out with a man and some adult conversation. But I got to worrying that it wouldn't work out, or maybe we would like each other. Or other teachers could find out about our going out, or one of the students could see us out. What kind of rumors would start going around? It's all so complicated. I hope he asks me out again, but I don't know what I would say if he did. Sometimes, I feel that I'm just as insecure about guys as the girls in my classes.

It's just so hard to meet eligible men when you're a female school teacher. Most of the teachers in high school are females; and the percentage is even worse in middle school, and especially in elementary school. I would really like to meet a great guy, fall in love, have kids, and build a life together as a family. Sometimes, I feel so empty inside about not having any of those things and wanting them so badly. I'm not even dating anybody; it's so depressing.

On the vast majority of days, though, I really, really love being a teacher. That's all I've ever really wanted to do—help kids; teach them neat things; get them excited about learning; teach this really exciting novel or play or short story, and the students get all excited about it and bring up points that I've never thought about; see the look on their faces when I tell them that they're teaching me something new about some work of literature I've read a thousand times.

Most of all, I live for those eureka moments when kids have been struggling and struggling to learn something; then all of a sudden, they get it. Maybe the kids couldn't figure out how to choose between a semicolon or comma, and I've corrected and corrected them. Then all of a sudden, they finally understand. I praise them, and they just show this little bit of a grin. And I know, I really know and believe then… that I'm a good teacher.

It's even better when some kid doesn't like to read at first and becomes a reader, then later still becomes a kid who I call a "lifetime learner." Luke is like that. I've taught him in both English 9 and 10 Honors and two years now in Yearbook, and he has changed so much. I've seen him go from a shy, unhappy boy to a young man with a future.

I've seen kids make bad mistakes and learn from them, like Marcus, and totally turn their lives around. He was a little jerk when I had him in ninth grade, then he started turning things around in tenth grade. Though I'm not teaching him this year, he comes by and chats with me before school about once a month. He's a young man now, too, not at all the spoiled little boy I met as a freshman.

But some of my students just can't seem to stop messing up. Like Luke, I've taught Elly all three years I've been here. I was so glad that she broke up with Caleb, a boy who will be nothing but trouble for whatever female he ends up with. I watched her make all these bad choices concerning guys for three years; and so many times, I would have liked to have counseled her about boys, but we really can't do that.

I see the way that Luke looks at Elly sometimes in Yearbook class, and sometimes I see her looking at him the same way when he's not watching. When they're working on a Yearbook spread together, there's a tenderness he shows toward her that's very touching. And I want to say to Elly, "Girl, grab this boy before he gets away from you." But, of course, I can't. Teachers have to be really careful about not interfering in students' personal lives.

I've taught girls like Mia who could end up with stellar careers in whatever field they go into. And I've taught girls like Mary who I hope don't get pregnant before graduation. I'd like to tell her that she needs to make better choices in life regarding boys and life, but how can I say something like that when my life is not the greatest?

I've got to stop beating myself up all the time about my teaching abilities and being so lonely. Maybe I should flirt with Mr. Martin the next time I have a chance. Maybe I should check out Match.com.

CHAPTER THIRTY-TWO
MIA'S MOM

He cheated on me. After 18 years of marriage and me being totally faithful to him, he cheated. I found out two weeks ago. He had been spending all this time on a computer... he kept saying that he was looking for jobs and filling out applications. For months now, I've been bringing in most of the money after he lost his Saturday job, and then his hours got cut back at the construction company.

He's been very distant to me lately, but I just thought it was because his pride was hurt because he wasn't making much money. I know we argued a lot over Mia and Luke dating, but he got what he wanted. They broke up because he wanted her to date a nice Hispanic boy. But even after we stopped arguing about that, we found plenty of other things to argue about. He even criticized how I looked, and said I had put on a few too many pounds.

Then came the night that changed everything. I was sewing in our living room late one evening. Mia came in, and she had this stunned look on her face. "You need to come see this," she said.

We walked into the den, and the computer was open to Instagram. I didn't even know he was into Instagram. And there were pictures of him and "Ann" doing things: out to eat, at the mall. "He's dating a white woman, how ironic is that?" said Mia. "After all that he put Luke and me through. He's cheating on you with a white woman. My father is an absolute pig."

I was just stunned. Mia said, "What are you going to do? Do you want to talk? Should we wake up the girls and tell them?"

I said, "I can't talk now. We can talk later. I just need to be alone and think. Go on to bed, sweetheart, and get your rest."

I went to the couch and just spent hours there, crying some of the time, furious some of the time. It was probably after 2:00 when I fell asleep. The only thing I had decided was that I wasn't going to spend that night sleeping in our bed with him.

The next morning, before work, I called our priest and asked if I could meet him after I got off duty at the hospital. He said yes; and that afternoon, I told him about what had happened. The first thing he asked was if I had done anything to displease my husband. That was not what I wanted to hear from my priest.

He then went on about the need for us to reconcile for the good of the family, and that he would be glad to counsel us. I told him that *I* was not the one who had been unfaithful, that *I* was not the one who had been cruel to our daughter, that *I* was not the one who couldn't hold down a job, and that *I* was not the one who had started all those arguments.

I kept all my anger and hurt inside for over a week, and tried not to act differently around him. I thought and thought about what to do. Maybe our priest was right about getting counseling. Maybe we should stay together because of the girls. But last Wednesday, when I got home from work, there was a message from him. He said he had gotten a call from the construction company, and that they needed him to come in to work; and one of the guys was picking him up and would bring him home.

I just didn't believe him, so I called the company. The man who answered said he wasn't supposed to work again until Friday... that things were still slow. When he came home around 8, I told him to get his stuff together and get out. "You can spend the night at Ann's house or on the street, it doesn't matter to me," I said. I told him we were through, and I would be hiring a lawyer and he should, too.

I'm not sorry I told him to get out. But it was tough telling Isabella and Emma that I had told their father to leave. "Why?" both of them kept saying. I didn't know what to tell them. Should I have gone into the details? I had told Mia not to tell them what was going on, and she hadn't. Isabella was really upset, and Emma was too... but not as badly. She's two years older, almost 11. Could she tell things weren't right in this house?

I was crying because I felt that he had wrecked our family. But Mia stepped in and said, "We're going to be alright. We'll get through this together." That girl, I'm so proud of her.

Later, when Isabella and Emma had gone to bed, Mia came into my bedroom and hugged me and said, "I'm glad he's gone. You can do better. You're going to be alright, and we're going to be alright. I love you so much. You're a great mama."

Yes, I can do better. Yes, I am a great mother. I'm only 35; I'm still young. I think I'm attractive. I could even meet a nice man and have more children, maybe have a boy this time. I can go back to school. I have my associate's degree in nursing, but I can go back and get my Bachelor of Science degree. It would be a struggle financially for two or three years, and there would be lots of long days. But getting more educated would lead to us having more money in the future, and more money for Isabella and Emma's education. Who knows... I might meet a really great guy while taking those courses.

One thing's for sure: we won't have a worthless male sitting around the house anymore, and we won't have to feed and clothe him. I have cried a lot since all that happened. But I feel better about myself than I have in a long time. I had to make a tough decision, and I made it. I'm moving on; my girls and I are moving on.

BREAKING UP/ GETTING BACK TOGETHER

CHAPTER THIRTY-THREE

LUKE

I broke up with Leigh after school on Wednesday. I wasn't planning to; it just happened. It started when she began talking about us going to prom in late April. I mean, it was mid-February; what was the rush? I told her I couldn't afford to go, which was the truth. I also said that if she wanted to go with somebody else, I wouldn't mind... that I would understand.

I thought saying something like that would make her feel good about our relationship, and that I was okay with her seeing other guys if she wanted to. Instead, she started crying. "Why don't you want us to be exclusive?" she kept saying. "Is there something wrong with me?"

"No, of course not," I said.

"No, you don't want us to be exclusive; or no, there's nothing wrong with me; or no for us being exclusive and yes for there being something wrong with me?" she replied, then cried some more.

By then, I was so confused about what to say and how to handle the situation, so I had this long pause. Meanwhile, she kept on crying. I finally responded that I realized she would probably be on the prom court; after all, she always has been. But I didn't want to go out on the gym floor and be her escort when we had the prom announcement assembly... that the whole thing would make me nervous. I also didn't want to dress up in a tux, besides not being able to afford renting one.

"Are you ashamed to be seen with me?" was her reply. I thought that was a low blow because she knows that's not true. I didn't know how to reply so it wouldn't hurt her feelings, so I again hesitated for a little while... which made her cry even harder. I tried to comfort her by patting her on the back and giving her a hug, but she just pushed me away.

"It's clear that you don't like me as much as I like you," she said. "Luke, don't you know how I feel about you?"

It's true what she said about how we feel about each other. For the longest time, I've worried about her being more into me than me into her. I do really like her, and it's more than just her great looks, but I just want something more from a relationship. I think there just comes a point in a relationship when you realize that you just don't click with someone— with Leigh, it was better than okay—but also that there's no long-term future there. It's just not good enough. Maybe it's even unfair to the other person to keep on going out; it's just dating for the sake of dating because that's what the two of you have been doing for a while.

Again, it was obvious that I had been doing too much thinking and not enough responding out loud to her because once more, she asked me if I realized how much she liked me.

I felt like she was trying to emotionally manipulate me, but I still didn't want to hurt her feelings. And I desperately needed some time by myself to figure out exactly what to say.

"Luke," she said. Her voice had a real edge to it like I had never heard before. "I need to know how you feel about me, and whether we are going to be exclusive or not. If not, we need to break up now."

"Then let's break up now," I blurted out. I was worn out from the whole discussion. I wanted to add that I hoped we could still be friends. It's true that I don't know much about girls; but I figured that if I said the friends thing, that would make her cry more or make her really angry. I just wanted to go home.

"I've got to go, bye," I said, and left it at that.

The worst part was not sleeping most of that night. I kept tossing and turning because of the whole breakup—what I said and what I should have said—and never came to any resolution. We sit next to each other in English and History; and I was worried all night, too, about how to deal with that. Should I go before school to Roche and Martin and ask them to let me sit somewhere else? What if they asked why or refused to move me? I was so screwed up about what to do with the seating thing that I ended up doing nothing.

Doing nothing turned out to be the right thing because when I got to both of those classes, she was already sitting somewhere else. For the next couple of weeks, she turned her head every time we passed in the hall. The third time she did it, I called her after school and apologized for the breakup, and said it was my fault. But I also told her it was just time for both of us to move on, and I hoped she found someone that she really liked.

"I appreciate you calling, Luke," she said. "I'm glad you did. I've started dating somebody else, and we're going to prom."

"Good for you," I said. "Have a great time."

We talked for a little while, I don't remember what about; and then we said goodbye. I was really, really glad I called her to clear the air. I was really glad that she got another boyfriend to take her to prom. I was super glad that boy wasn't me. I need to move on to somebody else, to get my grades up. I'm going to run five miles tomorrow morning before school and clear my head.

CHAPTER THIRTY-FOUR

ELLY

I had the best time on Saturday night, and it wasn't even a date. Late February means it's playoff time in basketball. Luke and I had to cover the first-round game—a home game—for Yearbook. He drove last time, so I came by his house and picked him up. He immediately began teasing me about my bangs being uneven, and wanting to know if one of my brothers was my new hair stylist. "It would be a great way to save money," he joked.

Then I started razzing him about how it was a good thing I was driving because his old pickup truck would probably have broken down before we got to the school's gym. The truck probably would still be stinky and gross from one of those deer he killed last fall. He laughed and said that at least his car had "character" and would be able to make it through snow, which was the forecast for the night. "What are you going to do, Miss Priss, if it starts snowing on the way home?" he asked. "Think your little blue Prius that your daddy bought for you can handle it?"

We joked like that all the way to the gym, and then we both got serious. He told me what kind of shots he wanted from the game, and I gave him some advice on who he should interview beyond the usual players and coaches. He really liked my idea about him going around and interviewing students in the stands and doing sidebars on all the energy in the air because it's a big playoff game. I'm not used to guys, especially the ones I've dated, listening to me when I make suggestions. I don't know much about basketball, but I've never heard the gym so loud before a game. It was like the student body was at some kind of rock concert.

As much as I hate sports, I've got to admit that even I got excited a few times. Quentin threw two behind-the-back passes to Matthew for dunks. And even though Matthew is a first-class jerk, I still screamed each time. Marcus kept hitting long shots; he must have made four or five treys, as Luke called them. We won by like 20 points, and I was so wound up from the game and being with Luke that on the way to drop him off, I pulled into a coffee house even though there was a chance of snow. He asked what I was doing, and I just said I was hungry.

Actually, I was hungry. But what I really wanted was for the evening not to end so soon. I'm still too thin from the binge-purging thing—how could I have been so stupid to do that and risk messing up my health? I ordered a bagel with my coffee, and Luke said he would have the same. One way or another, the subject got on who were the worst teachers we've ever had. He voted for Mrs. Burkhead, our freshman biology teacher, for her "ability to suck the life out of anything." I went with Miss Shaw, my tenth-grade gym teacher, who insisted that everybody could learn how to play golf. Then Luke started telling me funny stories about his temporary job as a Christmas tree salesman during the holidays. I especially liked the tale he told about a man asking him if there were any discounts coming up on the trees. Luke said he had wanted to tell the man they had a "two for the dollar sale on December 26," but had decided that kind of remark might get him fired.

Later, the subject turned to what our ideal life would be. I told him what I wanted most was a guy who would make me feel secure and cherish me, and would be a great dad for our children. Also, to become an elementary school teacher, and have a big house with a big lawn in the suburbs. He's the only guy I've ever had these types of discussions with.

"Well, three out of four's not bad," he said. "I hope your future husband likes spending all day every Saturday mowing that lawn."

"Maybe we could hire you to do it," I replied. "You certainly did a fine job when you used to mow our yard."

I was teasing when I said that, and then I got really upset with myself for suggesting that Luke would have to support himself by mowing other people's lawns, like my dad always said he would end up doing. To make up for saying that, I reached over and held his hand, squeezed it, and said, "I'm sorry, I didn't mean that in a bad way. I was just teasing."

"I know you didn't mean that," he said. "You have a really kind heart. I've known that for a long time about you, even when we were in middle school. And you know what? You're going to be a great wife, a great mom, and a great teacher."

After all I've gone through this year, I really needed to hear somebody say something like that. And he was sincere; Luke really does believe in me. Then I noticed that Luke and I were still holding each other's hand, and I didn't want him to let go. And I felt my face flush. I looked down at the table for a while; and when I looked up, Luke was staring at me like he was trying to say something, but didn't know how to say it.

Finally, he said something. "How would you feel if next Friday night, I came by your house around 7 in my smelly, gross pickup truck and took you out to eat at a nice restaurant? What would you to say to that?"

My heart started pounding so hard. The first thing I thought was what Mom and Dad would say, especially Dad. But then I remembered what Aunt Jenny had told me about following my heart. I said, "That would be really nice. I would really like that."

I squeezed his hand, and I felt him squeeze mine back, both strong and tender at the same time.

"Great," he grinned. "Well, it's late. You'd better drive me home."

I took out my phone, and it was late... past 11:00. We had been talking for almost two hours, and the time had just flown by. There were two texts (both from Dad), and the last one was "Where are you? Call me immediately!" Even worse, it had been snowing and the road was already covered, and I'd never driven in the snow. And my car doesn't have four-wheel drive.

I was in a panic and just started babbling about what we were going to do. Then Luke just took over.

"I've driven in the snow," he said. "I'll drive your car to your house and drop you off. Text your dad that you're on the way home and everything's okay. I'll walk home from your house; it's only three miles. Besides, it'll be good exercise, and I won't be able to run tomorrow if we get five or six inches. I don't want to call Granddaddy to come pick me up. He says he can't see well enough to drive in the dark anymore."

Just like that, everything was solved. Luke didn't have any problem driving me home. I felt so safe and secure with him. He made me laugh all the way home about all the dumb things that have happened to him in high school math classes. It was the best time I've ever had with a boy.

CHAPTER THIRTY-FIVE

MARCUS

School has never gone better for me than it has this year. But my sports life and love life haven't been so great, what with me sitting on the bench in football, my scoring average down three points in basketball, and Coach Henson saying I'd lost some of my quickness. And of course, Kylee breaking up with me hurt worse than anything. I've gone out with two other girls since then, but just once with each of them. There was zero chemistry both times.

But the way I played last Saturday night during the first round of regional playoffs made me feel like I had some of that old magic once more. I felt like I really contributed to my team. I made five treys, had three breakaway slams, went five for five from the free-throw line, and had 33 points overall. I tacked on 10 rebounds and five assists, too. The other starters and I didn't play most of the last quarter because we were so far ahead.

After the game, the assistant coach I met when I visited the university came up to me and said, "Nice game, Marcus, very impressive—especially the way you crashed the boards, dove on the floor, and passed the ball—those things don't show up in a box score. Keep in touch. Text me with updates on how you're doing."

I didn't even know he was there; he was probably at the

game to scout that stud center on the other team. Heck, I'm glad I didn't know Coach Ford was going to be there. I might have tensed up or tried to play outside of myself to impress him. It was then that I thought I should just put that great game and the meeting with Coach Ford out of my head. I figured he was going to be at the next playoff game on Tuesday night, given that Wilson has two guys that are D-1 material. And if I was staring into the stands and trying to spot Ford, it would hurt my game and make me look like an immature kid, too.

So I had my game face on all day at school on Tuesday. I went out and had another fantastic game, and we won another blowout. I wasn't as hot from the three-point line as last Saturday; but I still went four for nine there, hit all six of my free throws, and had another stat-stuffer line: 30 points, 11 rebounds, six assists, and even two blocks.

After the game, I saw that there was another text from Ford, asking if he could come to my house on Thursday after school to talk with me and my parents. Of course, I texted back immediately and suggested that he come for dinner at 6. He texted back quickly and asked me to ask guidance to fax him my grades. I know I didn't have to ask Mom if it was alright for Ford to come for dinner. When I met Mom and Dad after the game, she screamed when she found out the news. "Of course he can come for dinner," she yelled.

And Dad kept smiling and shaking his head up and down and saying, "Alright, alright, alright, my man."

On Thursday, Mom took a day off from work to make sure our maid cleaned the house perfectly in the morning, and to cook all afternoon. We had a huge dinner: prime rib, potato croquettes, salad, three vegetables, and pumpkin pie for dessert. Coach Ford raved about Mom's cooking. But even though everything was so great to eat, I could barely taste anything because I kept wondering if he was going to offer me a scholarship. After dinner, we all went to the living room;

and after thanking us for our hospitality, Ford said he would get straight to the point.

"We don't anticipate having any more scholarships available for your senior class, Marcus, as we've already had a really successful recruiting year," he said. "Your grades are fine, but some of those grades you had as a freshman will keep you from being eligible for an academic scholarship. And obviously, you all are too well-off to get a scholarship based on need.

"But what I can offer, and Coach Sullivan has approved based on my recommendation, is a spot on our team in your freshman year. You will be classified as a walk-on, but you won't have to compete as a walk-on to make the team. Then if things go well and your leg continues to heal and improve, which I think will happen, you will have a chance to earn a scholarship for your sophomore year."

Coach Ford emphasized again that he couldn't promise a scholarship, but I would have every opportunity to earn one by being a good teammate, giving 100 percent in practice, and making the most of my time on the court when I did get to play in a game. "I'm sure you all will need some time to discuss this among yourselves and get back to me," he said.

"No," I said. "I don't need any time. I want to come as a walk-on and go to the university."

Dad laughed at that, and Mom smiled. Then Dad said, "It's a fair deal. We'll take it."

I sent out texts that night to let everybody know that I was going to the university, and going to play as a walk-on. I got about 50 texts back that night, but the best ones were from Kylee and Mia. Kylee said that she was proud of me and that she was rooting for me to do well, and she knew that I would.

I've noticed her with three different guys since she broke up with me, all of them seniors. But what I've heard is that she hasn't been serious about any of them, and isn't seeing anybody or even in the talking stage with anybody now. I know she's thinking a lot about going to the university; and maybe sometime in the future, we could get back together. I know it's too soon now to even talk to her about eventually getting back together.

Mia's text was really nice, too. It said, "Congratulations, you'll love being a history major at the U. You might even be teaching there one day."

It was a pretty good week.

CHAPTER THIRTY-SIX

MIA

I was both relieved and stressed out when Mama kicked out my father. I was relieved that the constant bickering and fighting in our house was over. At first, I was worried about the loss of money from his construction job, but he was working so little and making so little money that I soon dismissed that fear. The stressful part was talking to Isabella and Emma about what had happened. How would they deal with not having their father in the house? Would it affect their grades, make them subconsciously rebel against Mama, and blame her for him being gone?

Mama told me she explained to my sisters why she decided to move on. But I knew they would still want to talk to me about what had happened. I told them it was wrong for him to have cheated on Mama. It was wrong for him not to try harder to find jobs. It was wrong for him to demand for us to wait on him hand and foot. Finally, I said, "Would you want to marry a man like that?" They both said no. Then I said, "Well, you can understand why Mama did what she did, then."

I told them to come talk to me whenever they were feeling down about him being gone, no matter how busy I was or what I was doing. He's been gone for two weeks now, and he hasn't even called to see how my sisters and I are doing.

I'm not surprised. And yes, I'm still mad about him breaking Luke and me up.

Elly called me on Sunday evening and said she wanted to come over to go for a walk—that she was desperate to talk to me. I figured she was having some sort of boy crisis again, so I said yes. After we left my house, she told me about what had happened.

She said that ever since she and Caleb had broken up, she had done everything she possibly could to avoid him. Her parents and Caleb's parents sit together at their church, so Elly had been volunteering to work in the nursery so as to avoid them and Caleb in Sunday school and church. But she had to face Caleb and his parents after church because her mom had invited them all over for lunch.

"I don't know if my mom and Caleb's mom planned the meal or Caleb put his mom up to it or whatever. But after lunch, Caleb asked me to go for a walk with him," Elly said. "He kept saying how sorry he was and that our breakup was all his fault... that he had changed, and that he wanted us to get back together and he would never cheat on me again. Then he said, 'I love you, Elly. Please give me another chance.'"

Elly said she didn't know what to say or do. Finally, she said she told him that she just didn't know whether she could ever trust him again. They walked and talked a lot more and when they got back to her house, she still didn't know what she was going to do and was being very noncommittal. When they came back inside, Elly said Caleb announced, "Elly and I are getting back together again."

"My parents and Caleb's parents both smiled, and they all said how wonderful that was and what a cute couple we are," said Elly. "Then Caleb said, 'Elly, how about we go out to dinner on Friday night to celebrate?' Everybody was smiling and looking at me. What was I supposed to say? So I said okay.

"Oh, Mia, I'm scared I made a big mistake. I'm still afraid of him. After Caleb and his parents left, Dad told me that he was so proud of me, that Caleb was the type of man who could provide for me and give me everything I deserve. All I could think of was that he was the type of man who would provide me with bruised wrists, black eyes, and broken ribs all the time while cheating on me."

Elly then broke down and just started bawling; she couldn't stop. I don't know how long we just sat there, with me comforting her. Finally, I said, "Listen to me. The first time he orders you around, let alone hits you or treats you rough, dump him. The first time, Elly, I mean it. You can do so much better. You deserve a great guy, but you've got to stop making these stupid decisions about guys. All the guys you've dated, they've been horrible for you."

"I know, I know," she said. "I promise, if Caleb...?"

"Not *if*," I interrupted, "*when* Caleb does something wrong, you will dump him."

We talked about that situation for another 10 minutes. Finally, she said, "How's your love life? Can I help you? As if I'm a fine one to offer advice."

I really did need to talk to someone about my love life. "You know Mateo, that senior from Wilson who's taking classes at the community college like I am?" I said. "Well, we finally had our first date last Friday night, went to a coffee shop and sat around and talked for a couple of hours."

"So how was it?" she asked.

"It was pretty good for a first date. A little awkward at first; then fine, okay, you know what I mean," I said. "We're going to a movie this Friday. So, we'll see."

Then I told Elly that I needed some advice from her about something I had been thinking really hard about. "I haven't talked to Luke since my father broke us up last year," I said. "Now that he's out of the picture, I'm thinking about calling Luke up, and just... hearing his voice again. Maybe asking him if he wants to go get coffee or something. What do you think about that?"

Elly had this really strained, bizarre look on her face

when I said that. Then she said in this strange tone, "Is that all you want? Do you want to try to get back together again with him?"

"I don't know what I want, or how Luke would feel if I did call," I said.

And that was really the truth.

CHEATING AND CENSORSHIP

CHAPTER THIRTY-SEVEN

LUKE

When Elly called me last Sunday night to tell me that she couldn't go out with me because she and Caleb had decided to get back together again, I was shocked and hurt—especially the hurt part. I've heard girls say that guys don't have feelings, but that's not true. Maybe we just hide how we feel and keep things to ourselves better.

Elly really, really hurt me. The times we've gone to cover sports events for the Yearbook, we've really had fun together. I love talking to her and being around her. I know she feels the same way. I really believe that. How could she prefer Caleb over me? That just doesn't make any sense. The way he treats her is disgusting. The way I've heard him talk about girls and brag about how smooth he is with women... I hate that type of guy.

I told Elly I understood that she couldn't go out with me. I didn't try to talk her out of it. Should I have? Sometimes, I worry that girls won't like me or go out with me because of my dad's criminal record, or my family always being poor. But America is supposed to be a classless society where anybody can be anything if they work hard enough. Is that true? Sometimes, I think it's true; and sometimes, I think it's crap. That's when I get like this gigantic chip on my shoulder. I get angry at myself and the world. But I don't want to be like that, feel like that, and live my life being angry. That's how Dad was all the time; he was always bitter and foul. No, I'm not going to be like that—like him.

I don't know how to handle this stuff that always seems to be happening with girls. I've dated quite a bit this year, more than I would have thought possible, especially since I was so shy and clueless as a ninth-grader. But I think that I'll just forget about the dating thing for the rest of this year and concentrate on school.

As if school was going so great. On Monday, Granddaddy and I had to meet with my guidance counselor, Mrs. Whitney, and the head of the special ed department, Mrs. Elliott, about my IEP—the old "individualized education program" for stupid-in-math students. Mrs. Roberts was there too to inform everyone that I had a *D* average in her remedial Algebra Functions class—"the gateway class," she said so that I would have the distinct honor of taking what was truly the most wonderful and fascinating class of all time, Algebra II. I dread taking that algebra crap in my senior year.

Mrs. Roberts was in full-blown teacher-speak mode, saying that I "possessed great potential" in math (which explains all those *D* and *F* grades), that I "was struggling temporarily with some of the harder algebraic concepts" (lady, on my good days, I can barely add and subtract), that perhaps Granddaddy "could go over my functions homework with me" (swell; Granddaddy told me he failed Algebra I in ninth grade and dropped out the next year) or perhaps he "could hire a tutor for Luke" (great, we'll just turn the heat off for a couple of weeks so we can afford a tutor who's not going to be able to help me, anyway).

The meeting ended with smiles and good spirits all around from Whitney, Elliott, and Roberts; a worried and confused look from Granddaddy; and me feeling more depressed than ever about the Elly thing and my math misery. I'm not knocking those teachers. Mrs. Whitney has always been nice to me, and so was Mrs. Elliott in the few times I've been around her. Mrs. Roberts is not a bad person; she just teaches an awful class with a bunch of stupid kids like me in it. No wonder she keeps saying she's going to retire in one more year. I mean, teaching math for a living? Who would be able to survive that for 30 years?

I was already feeling down when I walked into Ms. Roche's English 11 A.P. class on Tuesday. I felt even worse when I saw that she had this stern, pinched look on her face. I've learned that's never good when a teacher looks like that. It was the day we were supposed to get our major research papers back on *The Great Gatsby* and the Roaring Twenties. The kids in that room are smart—they could tell she was ticked by the way she was looking at us when we came in... the way she was drumming her fingers on her podium. Nobody was saying anything—the room was like hushed. And nobody said anything while she was handing out the papers. I got an *A-* on mine, which was about right. Like she wrote on my paper, I should have proofread it a few more times—that's on me. But I also noticed that about a half-dozen students didn't get their papers back.

"I spent most of last night grading your papers," she said as soon as the papers were handed out. "It seems obvious to me that quite a few of you plagiarized. Do you all realize that on the first day of school, each one of you signed the school's form on plagiarism? Do you all realize what you have put me through? The hours of checking up on your sources. The hours of agonizing over whether or not you intentionally plagiarized or just didn't follow directions.

"Agonizing over how I would explain things to you. Agonizing over how you would react. How I would explain an *F* to your parents. Agonizing over whether you deserved another chance when I really didn't think you did. Do you realize that in the real world, the adult world, there are serious consequences when you steal someone else's work? Again, did some of you even for a second realize what you put me through!?"

All of a sudden, Caleb interrupted Miss Roche and said, "You can't prove that I plagiarized. I want my paper back now."

"Don't interrupt me," Miss Roche shot right back. "I am not going to discuss any student's grades in front of the class."

It was about that time that Caleb began "elaborating" on Miss Roche's similarity to a female dog, followed by Miss Roche strolling over to the upper right drawer of her desk, where most teachers seem to keep their discipline referral forms. It was the high point of my week, watching Caleb slam the door and head for Mr. Caldwell's office. Yep, Elly, you made the right move preferring him to me.

CHAPTER THIRTY-EIGHT

ELLY

I should never have gotten back together with Caleb. Why do I keep making the same mistakes over and over with boys? On our first date, everything went well, oh, for about 15 minutes or however long it took for him to drive us to the restaurant and for us to order our meal. I ordered flounder and a baked potato with butter and sour cream. After the waitress left, he criticized me for wanting both butter and sour cream. He said I shouldn't put both of them on the potato—that he didn't want me "getting fat" again.

For the first time ever, I started to argue with him, telling him that I was just now starting to recover from doing some very unhealthy things. He had promised me he had changed and wasn't going to boss me around about everything. That little remark caused him to raise his voice toward me, saying, "Don't you argue with me out in public, woman!" He was so loud that I just knew people at the nearby tables heard every word and were staring at us.

I was so angry at him and mad at myself that I barely ate anything, especially that stupid potato. Caleb sat there across from me, stuffing himself and not caring that he had really upset me. Then I started thinking that this night could have been my first date with Luke. He would have had me laughing, and we would have been talking about all kinds of things at a restaurant that would have been about half as expensive as this one.

Next, I just started to cry... not those loud, heaving sobs that I sometimes have, but just these little tears that kept dribbling down my cheeks. "I could have been out with Luke, I could have been with Luke this instant," I kept thinking. The more that thought kept repeating itself, the more the tears fell.

I know I really hurt Luke when I called him to say that Caleb and I were back together. He could have lashed out at me or said something sarcastic, but he just kept saying that he understood. But his voice was not right; it was sort of strained, low, and... sad. Sooner or later, I know Caleb and I are going to break up again. As soon as I get a little more self-respect and finally grow up and act like I have some sense... that's when.

But what I really worry about is that I've blown it forever with Luke. He's asked me out twice, and I've turned him down both times—the second time was much worse than the first time last fall. He'll think he can do better than me. I really fear that he'll think that. Why on earth wouldn't he? Few guys would ask a girl out a third time after being turned down twice, right?

When it came time for dessert, Caleb ordered apple pie a la mode. Then he stared at me, as if daring me to order something. And I just said to the waitress, "Coffee, please, black." I wasn't going to get into it again with him in public.

When we got back to his car, the first thing he did was get out some sort of rum from under his seat.

"If you take one swallow of that, I swear I'm getting out of the car," I said. "I'm not bluffing."

He cursed at me, then said he was going to take me straight home, and that the night was still "young." I started to say something smart back, but I am so scared of his temper that I decided to just shut up. Besides, he was driving me straight home, and I could care less if he was going to go visit one of his other girlfriends or drink himself into a stupor.

I had my hand on the door handle as soon as we pulled onto our street, and I shot out of that car as it was rolling to a stop. I ran up the steps to our house in no time, and I heard Caleb roar off. As soon as I came inside, there were Mom and Dad; and she beamed, just beamed, "Have a good time? You're home early."

"Fantastic," I said. "I had a little headache, so he dropped me off."

When I got to my room, I thought once again about calling Luke. I even started to, but I just couldn't make myself do it. I wish Luke could afford a cell phone. Then I could have texted him about some assignment or something and seen how he responded. Maybe I could go on from there to text about other things, or maybe even convince him to call me. What's the matter with me that I can't screw up the courage to do the right thing and call him and apologize for breaking our date, and ask him to give me another chance?

On Tuesday, in class, it was humiliating to be sitting next to Caleb when Ms. Roche busted him for plagiarism. But I was glad that she did. He had bragged over dinner that he had "put one over on her." I wonder which one of his little tarts wrote the paper for him? Sure as the world, he didn't. Paige looked at me and shook her head when Caleb stormed out of the room; and after class, she came up to me and said, "Elly, you've got to break up with him."

"I know, I know," I said.

We're supposed to go out again this Friday, and I suggested—insisted—that he come to my house so I could fix him a dinner of all his "favorite things." If he starts criticizing me and raising his voice, I want my parents to hear the way he talks to me. If I'm smart, I'll break up with him then. I definitely don't want to go anywhere in a car with him.

CHAPTER THIRTY-NINE

MARCUS

After all that arguing at the beginning of the year about my English 11 A.P. class maybe reading *Huck Finn*, we finally started reading it this week. That slang language people spoke back in the day was really hard to get used to; but once I got the hang of it, the story was so powerful. A black slave is floating down the Mississippi River with this poor white kid. They're encountering all these people who show "the best and worst of our human nature, mostly the worst," said Miss Roche—she's right about that.

We're reading most of the book on our own, usually five or six chapters a night. Then we discuss it in class the next day with Miss Roche asking us to read out loud passages that we felt were especially important. One day, I read out the beginning of a passage in Chapter 6: "There was a free n— there, from Ohio; a mulatter, most as white as a white man..." When I read out the N-word, Miss Roche got this horrified look on her face and said, "You didn't have to read out the N-word. You can just skip over it if you want."

"No," I said, "reading it makes the passage more powerful. I swear—this is the most powerful book I've ever read. Twain is absolutely ripping the white hypocrisy of the time."

I went on to say that Pap, Huck's father, actually thinks while he is talking in this passage that he is better than this partially black dude because the man has a little bit of black blood in him. Pap can't read or write, and is all bent out of shape that this black man can be a professor and vote—that the man doesn't "know his place." Then I read out the end of the passage, where Pap is so mad about that man voting that Pap said, "Thinks I, what is the country a-coming to? It was 'lection day, and I was just about to go and vote, myself, if I warn't too drunk to get there." I said that was absolutely hilarious and awesome satire at the same time.

Luke then spoke up and agreed with me, which I really appreciated, and said it was one of the two or three best books he had ever read along with *Walden* and *1984*. Luke said that both the poor whites and blacks were victims of a feudal-like system in the South. And if the whites had ever been smart enough to have figured it out, there wouldn't have been so much racial and social injustice for so long. I was really glad that Luke saw some of the same things in the book that I did. I was also really glad that Caleb had been suspended for three days for the little run-in he had had with Miss Roche. He would have been inserting his racist crap into the whole discussion.

Later, a couple of white students said reading and seeing the N-word made them uncomfortable. And I had to explain once again that I wasn't offended. Thankfully, Kylee agreed with me, and she felt that it was "extremely important" that we read *Huck Finn* and that it not be censored here like at a lot of other schools. Camila then said that the attitude whites had toward blacks back then was similar to the way that some people today feel about people like her who are Hispanic. Camila was really wound up about this. I was impressed by how she was talking straight from the heart. All in all, it was one of the best discussions I've ever been involved in.

At lunch, I was still so excited about English class that when I saw Camila carrying her tray through the cafeteria, I walked over to her and asked if she wouldn't mind sitting down with me and talking about what happened in class. We ended up discussing the book until the bell rang. We were talking so intensely that neither one of us had time to finish our lunch. After the bell rang, I told her that I had really enjoyed talking to her; and she said the same.

I suddenly had all this guilt about how immature I had been as a freshman when we were dating, and I said, "I just wanna apologize about how I was such a jerk when we were dating in the ninth grade."

She laughed and said, "Well, I was pretty immature, too. You weren't the only one in the relationship who needed to grow up. We were both probably too young to be dating each other."

I walked her to our next class, and we talked the whole way there. These thoughts started rushing into my head that she was a girl I should try to get to know better. I thought about asking her out right then, but that type of sudden impulse was often what got me into trouble in the past. So, I decided to just put the brakes on to keep myself from doing something stupid.

That night, though, I got a text from her about a *Huck Finn* passage in Chapter 15 she had just read for homework. It was the one where Huck apologizes to Jim for having pulled a mean trick on him. She asked me what I thought it meant. I had already read the homework chapters that Miss Roche had assigned, so I texted back that I thought the meaning was that Huck was beginning to realize that blacks had feelings just like anybody else—a unique realization for the time period. We must have texted back and forth a dozen times over that topic before I went to bed. Yes, I'm going to take it slow with her the second time around.

It was good that school was so interesting this week because my basketball season came to a crushing end on Friday night. We had to go on the road to play against a really good team, Monroe; and they blew us out of their gym. I only scored eight points and shot about 30 percent. The guy that Monroe put on me was two inches taller, and had already gotten a free-ride scholarship from a D-I school. He was also a lot quicker than I was; and all night, he either drove around me or shot over me. I just couldn't stay with him. It was a good reminder of why I should be thankful to be a walk-on when I go to college.

CHAPTER FORTY

MIA

I wish I were in Miss Roche's first-period English 11 A.P. class. We only have 12 people in my seventh-period class because it consists of students who either are going to STEM in the morning or taking college classes in the first part of the day like me. Luke's in the morning class; and so are a lot of my best friends like Elly, Paige, and Camila. The other day, Miss Roche started the class off with the racism issues that the novel *Huck Finn* brings up and what her morning class had discussed and argued about.

But my class seemed reluctant to talk about those issues. Was it because ten of us are girls? Are we less confrontational than boys, or is that just a stupid stereotype? Or is it because so many people in our room are STEM kids and are more into science and math than English? I don't know.

I do know that *Huck Finn* is one the most powerful books I've ever read. I loved the ironic passage in Chapter 16 where Huck worries about the morality of stealing Miss Watson's slave when people back then were so unconcerned about morality that they enslaved millions of people.

I was thinking so much about how Luke would have commented on the book that I decided to do something spur-of-the-moment—which definitely is not like me. I decided to wait for him at the school's front entrance like I did all of last year… when we gave each other a goodbye kiss before we got on our buses. When he walked out the door, he saw me immediately and seemed confused about whether to stop or not, or just nod and walk on by—which is what he has done all year because of my father's orders for me not to have any contact with him. Well, Daddy is out of the picture now; and if I want to talk to Luke, I'm going to do it.

"Hi," I said. For the first time ever, I felt awkward around him and at a loss for words.

"Hey," he said and stopped. He looked just as confused as I probably did.

"Do you have time to go somewhere and talk?" I said.

"Yeah, I've got the truck today," he said. "I can drive you home. I heard about your mom and dad splitting up."

"Let's go to the coffee shop," I offered.

"No, how about the Dairy Queen, just like old times?" he said with a touch of a smile.

It was incredibly awkward getting in that old red pickup of his once again. On the way there, I felt that the air was heavy with unspoken thoughts. Neither one of us said anything. Was he feeling awkward around me, too? I never would have thought that would ever be possible.

We ordered ice cream cones (his—the usual vanilla; mine—the usual chocolate), and sat down. Still, neither one of us said anything.

Finally, I spoke up. "I'm so sorry about how I handled breaking up with you last year. I know I hurt you. I know you wanted us to secretly date; but I just couldn't do that with the way things were between my parents, and the promise I made to my dad about not having anything to do with you.

"But my father didn't keep the promises he made to Mama about their marriage vows, so I don't owe him anything anymore. And I just wanted to say I'm sorry I hurt you."

"Mia," he said. "You did hurt me; it really hurt. It hurt all summer and into the fall until school started, and I couldn't get other things off my mind. But I want you to know I was never mad at you. I just…"

And there was this long pause. "Just what?" I said, trying not to cry.

"I just was disappointed in you, that's all," he said.

A guy could have said he was angry at me. Or a guy could have said that he hated me for something I did or said. But Luke just saying he was *disappointed* in me… that hurt worse than anything any boy or girl has ever said to me.

"You had every right to be disappointed in me," I said. Then a few tears welled up and rolled down my cheeks. "I'm not a crier," I said.

"No, you're not," he said. "You're about the strongest, most self-confident person I've ever met. I can't tell you how much you meant to me and how you changed my life around, helping me to become more self-confident, helping me make up my mind to go to college… making me see that I was worth something… that I was worthy of somebody like you, being there for me through Mom's cancer and when Mom and Dad died last year within months of each other. You even brought me something to eat when everything was out of whack at home. I'll never forget what you did for me. I'm very, very grateful for you."

Grateful enough for us to try to get back together? I thought. But did he want that, did I want that, had I hurt him too deeply? If we got back together now, would we stay together when I go away to college? From what I've heard, he's going to the small liberal arts college in the county.

I wanted him to say something, but then I realized he had finished his thought and was waiting for me to reply.

"Maybe we can get together some other time soon and talk some more?" I said.

"I'd like that," he said.

Then I asked him to drive me home. I had hours of homework to do.

STRESSED TO THE MAX

CHAPTER FORTY-ONE
LUKE

Too much has been going on lately, and I feel stressed out. The other day after school, Mia and I talked for the first time since she broke up with me. We went to get ice cream; and I felt all these weird, conflicting feelings. I was glad to just be near her again, but I'm still hurt from the breakup. I'm wondering why she wanted to talk to me, but not really understanding why she would. Did she want for us to try to get back together, or I was just too clueless to pick up on her real intentions?

Would I like to get back together with her when we would probably have to break up again when she goes far away to college? Or maybe because we were so good together when we were dating—we had such a great relationship—that we would have an even better one now that we are older? Perhaps together, we could overcome any obstacles—she is a superior woman. I just don't know. I'm not going to make the next move with her—that's just too stressful. I broke up with Leigh this spring, Elly broke what would have been our first date in order to get back together with that punk Caleb, Mia asking to talk to me... It's all too much too close together. I'll just wait and see what happens and what Mia might do next. Maybe nothing; maybe she just wanted to talk, and that was really all to it.

I've got enough to worry about on the home front. Something's not right with Granddaddy. Every first of April, he has always planted a garden. This year, he said he didn't think he would "fool with one." He said he had been so tired lately. That's just not like him; the garden has always been his big thing for the spring and summer, even when he was still working a job.

He also seems really forgetful lately. Maybe it's nothing, but what if it's dementia or something like that? The other day, after I got home from school, he said he was going to the grocery store, which is just down the road. He still wasn't home almost two hours later, and I was starting to get really worried. Then I got a phone call, and he said he must have made a wrong turn and gotten lost. He was on Branch Street. Then he asked if I knew where that was.

I had never heard of Branch Street, so I decided I'd better call the police and ask for their help in finding him. When I called, the woman on duty said that Branch Street was in the next county over; and that she would send someone to help him find his way home. Granddaddy could follow an officer home. I told her I was very grateful for her help.

It was over an hour before Granddaddy got home, and it was well past dark. I asked the officer what took them so long, and he said that Granddaddy seemed disoriented and was following him real slowly all the way to our house. Then the policeman said, "Should your grandfather still be driving? I'm not sure that he should. This getting-lost thing could be the start of a serious problem."

What am I supposed to do about that? How is a 17-year-old kid supposed to tell an 81-year-old man that he can't drive anymore? But what if the officer was right about him being too old to drive? What if Granddaddy was in a wreck and hurts some family with young kids in the car? I would be responsible for that happening. I could hide the keys from him, but that really wouldn't solve anything long-term.

School has just added another layer of stress to everything

else. Until I took Chemistry, I would sometimes think I might want to major in science. I hated taking Biology with Mrs. Burkhead; but I love learning about plants and animals, and I absolutely loved my Ecology class last year. But that *D* average in Chemistry I looks like it's never going to get any higher, and all that math stuff in that class is just absolutely awful.

Take, for instance, the word *stoichiometry*. The other day, Mrs. Wilson said that stoichiometry "is all about the proportions between atoms in molecules and reactants/ products in chemical reactions. You all will now be able to balance chemical equations." My mind flashed back to trying to balance equations in math classes, and what a disaster that always was. Equations never balance out—that is an absolute fact. They are not supposed to balance out because you will absolutely be driven insane before they would ever balance out.

My mind was still trying to wrap itself around those long sentences of hers and trying to get a grasp on the balancing crap. But she was already through with that topic, and was racing at full speed toward "balancing redox reactions." What is *redox*? Does it have something to do with oxygen, or is it carbon dioxide? I was so stressed out from that, I just shut down for the rest of the class. I wanted to raise my hand to get some help, but I'm tired and embarrassed of continually asking questions in there. Mrs. Wilson goes too fast, and she almost never comes around to our desks when we're balancing stuff to check how we are doing individually.

With that woman, it's just lecture, lecture, lecture; test, test, test; then moving warp speed onto the next impossible-to-understand topic. She says we've got to "cover concepts" in preparation for the Chemistry state test in late April. I wonder when the *expedited retakes* for that test will be, and who my tutor will be. Maybe I'd better find out who teaches the class in summer school. My stomach feels that it's got a knot the size of a basketball in it.

CHAPTER FORTY-TWO
ELLY

Caleb was scheduled to come to my house for dinner at 7:00 on Friday night; but by Wednesday, I had made up my mind about what I was going to do. I was going to break up with him permanently after dinner. But before that, I was going to talk to my parents and finally come clean to them about their beloved Caleb.

As soon as Dad got home around 5:30, I told him and Mom that we had to talk right now.

"Shouldn't you be working on Caleb's dinner?" asked Mom.

"Fixing his dinner won't take 15 minutes," I said, and she had a puzzled look when I said that. "All I'm fixing is scrambled eggs, and some leftover rolls from last night. He should be gone by 7:30. Would you and Dad sit down—now!"

We went over to the couch, and I started ranting. "I'm breaking up with Caleb permanently tonight, and there's no talking me out of it. I'm ashamed of myself to be with him, or even to have my name associated with his. He's been suspended from school several times this year, kicked off the football team, and..." I paused for a long time. "He's tried to get me drunk with him, he's driven drunk, he's hurt me physically, he's been abusive emotionally. I'd lost all my self-respect, and I'd just started to get back some of it after I broke up with him the first time.

"Then he manipulated me into giving him another chance. And that was a huge mistake. I don't care about how much you two like him; he's a horrible, horrible person, and he's never going to change."

Mom said, "I wish you had told us before that he was hurting you. I don't want you ever to go out with those types of boys."

Then Dad said, "I agree 100 percent with your mother. It's just that we're such good friends with his parents, and his dad and I..."

I would never have believed that I would have interrupted my father. But I was at the end of my rope, and he did not have the right to excuse away Caleb's behavior. "Your relationship with them is not more important than you being a good father to me, is it?" I asked. "You don't really want me being with, or ever marrying someone, who physically and emotionally abuses me, do you? It's not just me saying these things about Caleb. I didn't kick him off the football team. I didn't get him suspended from school. I didn't make him cheat on tests, or plagiarize on papers. I did nothing to make him cheat on me and go out with all those other girls. I'm not the reason he abuses alcohol."

Dad just sat there with this stunned look on his face. I don't think he expected that kind of attack from his "sweet little girl."

Finally, Mom said something. I just could have hugged and kissed her. "I support your decision," she said. "I knew Caleb had been kicked off the football team, but his mother told me it was all a big misunderstanding. I don't want you to be with a boy like that. You can do better."

"Dad, do you wanna say anything?" I asked.

"I apologize for pushing you to be with him and giving him another chance," he finally said. "Yes, you break up with him, sweetie. And if he gives you any problems when he's here, just raise your voice and I'll be there."

"Thank you, thank you both," I said. In the past, I would probably have cried when I said that; but my mind was all set on Caleb coming through the door soon. For one of the few times in my life, I felt strong and confident—really sure of myself. It was going to be really stressful when he came, sat down and ate; but I knew I finally had my act together. I was in charge.

When Caleb rang the doorbell, I purposefully made him wait for about two minutes. I had dressed in an old pair of jeans and tennis shoes. I had a black blouse on, had my long brown hair in a tight bun, and I wasn't wearing any blush or eyeliner. I wanted to look like an angry, severe woman, not a star-struck, vulnerable girl.

"I'm ready to start dinner," I said to him. "Come on back to the kitchen and sit down."

I scrambled up one egg, heated up yesterday's rolls, plopped everything on his plate, gave him a plastic spoon and no fork, sat down, and said, "Your dinner's served. I think *you need to lose some weight*—so just one egg for you. I'm eating my egg frittata later."

"I'm not taking you out to dinner, if that's what you're trying to pull," he said.

"Fine, no going out to dinner," I snapped. "Eat up."

He tore into his food, and it was obvious how pissed off he was at me. When he had finished, I said, "Get out of my house. I'm never going out with you again. You're a terrible person. And you're not to spread rumors around school about me, or write things on social media about me. If you do, and I find out about them, I'm going to tell Dad; and I'm going to report you to the school resource officer. Get out!"

He called me a bitch like he usually does, and added in a few of his other favorite curse words. All I said was "Get out now, before I have to call my father. He said he'd be close by if I needed him."

As soon as Caleb stormed out, I texted Mia, Paige, Camila, and Kylee and gave them, shall I say, "an abbreviated summary" of my last "date" with Caleb. Mom and I then made fudge brownies and stuffed ourselves. It was one of the best nights of my life.

CHAPTER FORTY-THREE

MARCUS

I'm not working out in the weight room this spring because I'm done with football. I'm not dating anyone—although Camila and I are definitely in the talking stage; and soon, maybe more. All that is probably good because school couldn't be more stressful and it's sucking up all my time. I feel I've got to make up this year for all those low grades I had back in freshman year. I've got to make an *A* in everything this semester to prove to myself and my parents that I can do really, really well in college.

The hardest subject by far is Honors Chemistry, and it's the only subject I don't have an *A* in. It's a very shaky *B* right now. That stoichiometry stuff is bad enough, but dimensional analysis seems way over my head sometimes. It's all about these relationships with physical quantities, which is bad enough; but then it's got all these things called "fundamental dimensions." And those things have got all these qualities like length, electric charges, mass and time. Plus, mixed in with that are all these units of measurement, kilo this and kilo that... miles, pounds, grams, and so on. You've got to do calculations and consider dimensions. It's layer after layer of all this stuff and it's all supposed to fit together, but it really doesn't. I guess Mrs. Wilson is a good teacher; she sure seems to know what she' s talking about. But being in there sometimes just makes my head feel like it's going to split apart. Some of the smartest kids in school are struggling in there.

History is the highlight of my day just about every day. I really love doing those projects Mr. Martin assigns and that we have to present to the class. Luke and I have been paired up all year. We like to take a topic and make it controversial. He gets a kick out of that, and so do I.

The last one we did was creating an alternate timeline if Germany had won World War II and America became a second-rate power. We had Hitler living up to 1964; the Civil Rights movement never happening; certain presidents never becoming president; and World War III beginning in 1984 and ending in a nuclear holocaust in 1985, with most of the world being destroyed. Then in the 1990s, the survivors were trying to cobble together some kind of society in what was left of this country. But even then, the far left and far right couldn't compromise. It was so cool. Luke and I took our alternate universe right up to the present times, with both the East Coast and the West Coast uninhabitable, and five million Americans are left trying to survive in the Great Plains region. A third of them wanted a strongman ruler, a dictator who would remilitarize and get revenge on Hitler's successors. A third of the people wanted to restore a Constitution-based government. The last third just wanted to be left alone and be survivalists. Martin said it was one of the best projects he had ever had anybody present.

Luke and I made our presentation last Friday. After school that day, Camila texted me and said how impressed she was with what we had done. We texted back and forth four or five times, and this thought popped into my head that it was a Friday and she was sitting alone at home. I had worked really hard all week and could use some time out of the house and away from studying. I just kept thinking: was Camila starting to get interested in me, or maybe she was just being friendly? How would she take it if I texted her about meeting for coffee?

I finally got up enough courage to just go for it. I texted, "R u up for goin' out for coffee?"

Like 15 seconds later, she texted back, "Where and when?" A half hour later, we were sitting at the local coffee shop. She's really smart; and obviously, she's always been great-looking. Of course, when we were ninth-graders, all I cared about was the great-looking part. I never bothered to get to really know her.

But Camila has all these really strong opinions, and she's not shy about expressing them. I actually like that about a girl now. That's the way Mom is, and Dad certainly has no complaints. He's told me that's one of the things he admires most about her. The first thing Camila and I started talking about was the History class project. She said she loved the whole thing, but there was one part she would have done differently. I had to ask her what part that was.

"What if, in the twenty-first century, you had America begging for Central and South Americans to emigrate to the country so that the United States could be repopulated?" she said. "There were more people down there than up here because those countries had been neutral during the nuclear war. But nobody wanted to come to the United States because it was so unstable because all the factions couldn't agree on anything."

I had to admit to her that that was a fantastic concept, and it would have been great to have been part of the project. We then talked about religion and politics and all those things that never came up when we were dating the first time. The next thing I knew, four hours had passed, and it was close to 11:00.

"Would you like to go hang out next Friday night, maybe go out to dinner?" I asked.

"I'd like that very much," she said.

Not a bad way to end a week.

CHAPTER FORTY-FOUR

MIA

I knew that the second semester of those college classes I'm taking every morning was going to be rough; but I had no idea that they would be this hard, time-consuming, and stressful. Sometimes, I only get four hours of sleep a night; and most nights, I only get five. Around about midnight every night, I start nodding off, and I find myself actually falling asleep for a few minutes every now and then. Around 1:00, I come to my senses long enough to realize that I'm still on the same page of some textbook that I was reading an hour ago. Then I realize I might as well go to bed because I can't hold my head up anymore.

All night long, I toss and turn because every time I wake up just for a little bit, I feel guilty and worried that I'm not studying. I look at the clock and it's 5, and I feel I'd better get up because I have some sort of big test at 8, and I'd better look over those notes again or I won't be prepared for what's coming up. Every day is like this, and it goes on week after week.

BIO 142 (Human Anatomy and Physiology II) is probably the hardest class. It's such an important class for me to excel in to become a doctor. The course is mainly about integrating the concepts of chemistry, physics, and pathology. We have three hours of lecture and three hours of lab every week.

The lectures are non-stop note-taking; and the professor never stops talking or asks questions, or ever checks for understanding. How could he? The room is crammed full of people and most of them are actually college students.

Mateo sits next to me in that class, and it makes me feel good that he feels overwhelmed in there, too. Misery does love company, they say. We're both making an *A* in there, but we agree that neither one of us can see how that is happening. After class, we almost always get a quick cup of coffee because there's a half-hour to kill before our next class, Principles of Psychology. It's not as hard as BIO 142, but it's harder to keep things straight… if that makes any sense. For example, one of the lectures last week was on physiological mechanisms, and touched on psychopathology. It was physio this and psycho that for the whole hour of lecture time.

The morning ends with HLT 144 (Medical Terminology II). It's the easiest of the three classes, but it still involves reading technical stuff for 90 minutes every night; and those projects every two weeks are brutal. My high school classes are a breeze compared to the college ones, but adding all of them together is about more than I can handle on most weeks.

I got voted onto the prom court this week, which was ironic considering that I hadn't planned to go, can't afford a dress, and really don't have a steady boyfriend. Mateo and I have gone out three times, just casual dates where we've gone out to a movie or for coffee. The third time, we went to play Putt-Putt. I hadn't hit a golf ball since P.E. in tenth grade; and frankly, it is not one of my favorite things to do in life. Talk about a nothing sport.

But I really enjoyed mindlessly knocking a hot pink ball into obstacles for 45 minutes. I was so bad at hitting the ball that Mateo held my arms and tried to position them so that I could actually "address the ball" correctly, as he said. That was the first time he's actually touched me. He hasn't kissed me or held my hand yet. I think he's trying to work up his nerve to do so. He's a little bit of a nerd, but that's okay. I don't have time to be in a complicated dating relationship right now; and I don't have the inclination, either. Maybe he feels the same way because of all the stress he is under, with a heavy load of high school and college classes.

Somehow, Mateo found out that I was on the court. He asked me if I needed an escort, which seems about as romantic as he is capable of. No elaborate promposals from this boy, just a "Do you need an escort? I could take you if you need one."

I didn't want to hurt his feelings by rejecting him, but I didn't feel like I had time to waste on going to a four-hour dance, either. Obviously, my family doesn't have the money for me to buy a prom dress. So to get out of the whole awkward situation, I said I would have to ask my mom if we could afford a dress.

I figured Mama would say no about the dress, but she said we could go to one of those formal dress shops and at least check out what girls are wearing. She said that with my father gone, the food bill was considerably less; and since he wasn't bringing in any money anyway, we were actually doing better financially. I figured that was the case.

So Mama and I went dress shopping on Saturday, and I picked out something that I would like to wear if we could have afforded it. Then, to my surprise, Mama said she could make something like that dress for a fraction of the cost; and just like that, I was going to prom. Mama said one of our neighbors down the street owes her a favor, and the woman works at one of those boutique shops, so she can do my hair and nails. Imagine that: me going somewhere at night, and I won't be dressed in jeans and a blouse.

PROM WEEK

CHAPTER FORTY-FIVE

LUKE

With the stress of school and all the stuff I've gone through with dating this year, I could hardly wait for the overwhelming joys of "prom week." All during the week of prom, before the "gala event of the century" on Saturday, we were treated to announcements about deadlines to buy tickets, the prom court assembly, and instructions on what to do if you were bringing a date who doesn't attend this school. Oh, the thrill of it all.

A week before the big day, two girls even asked me to take them to prom. One was a desperate sophomore named Sandy who lives down the street from me. I've never even had any classes with that girl and I don't know anything about her, and she expects me to spend gosh knows how much money on her for a one-time date at a place where I don't want to be. I can't dance; I've got no rhythm. I don't want to be there. Amber, who I went out with like once back in the fall, asked me out, too. I turned her down. We had a real dud of a date; why go on another one with her?

Leigh was named prom queen; good for her. I'm glad that she's got another boyfriend now. When I was coming into English class the other day, I stopped by and congratulated her. I'm glad that we can still be friends after our breakup. I was happy for Mia that she was placed on the court. Good for her, too. I hope she also has a date for it.

The way I prepared for prom weekend was packing a backpack on Thursday night. I put in a tent, sleeping bag, mess kit, first aid kit, water purifier, mini-propane stove, and a copy of *Huck Finn*. I also threw in some freeze-dried meals, oatmeal packets, four potatoes, salt and pepper, and dried fruit. With a Buck knife in a sheath, fly box in a pocket, and a pack fly rod, I was ready to head for the mountains. My goals were to live like a mountain man for a few days, catch a lot of brook trout, and eat a couple of them; finish reading *Huck Finn* for English class; and be alone with my thoughts.

I rode my bike to the national forest, chained it to tree well off the road, and hiked to a spot about two miles back where I like to camp. The spot is right next to a native brookie stream and about a hundred yards off the trail, so I knew I wouldn't have any visitors. I found this spot just by luck a couple of years ago. I was wading upstream and fishing for trout; and when I waded around a bend, there was this really neat natural opening. I've come back to it several times since then to spend the night. I even took Mia there on one of our dates last year. She loved the spot. Rhododendron grows along the banks, and so do speckled alders and basswood.

About an hour before dark, I set up camp. I went down to the stream and tied on a Size 14 Adams; and thirty minutes later, I had caught two seven-inch or so trout. I don't usually like to eat native brook trout. They symbolize wild nature to me in how they live in these isolated mountain streams that are way away from civilization. But sometimes, I just like to have that entire wilderness experience of not just being out in the middle of nowhere, but also being a part of it in some kind of special way. Eating a wild trout out in the middle of nowhere is an amazing part of the overall experience. I know this won't make sense to a lot of people, but it makes perfect sense to me.

I don't like to build fires in the national forest because

those rings seem to last forever. I don't like for my camping spot to look like anybody has ever been there. So I used my propane stove first to boil the two trout. After I cooked and ate them, I cut up the potatoes and boiled them. With the salt and pepper, they tasted great.

The next morning, I let the songbirds wake me up. I heard Carolina wrens, wood thrushes, and scarlet tanagers. The last two have just migrated back here to nest, and it was good to hear them singing again. I cooked oatmeal on the stove, adding in some dried cranberries, and had a very filling breakfast.

After breakfast, I waded upstream and fished until about 11:00. I must have caught 20 wild trout on the Adams. Brook trout aren't hard to fool with a fly, you just have to wade softly and sneak up on them. Then if you make an accurate cast into one of those wash basin-sized pools, you'll usually catch one.

I came back to camp, ate a couple of energy bars, and took a long two-hour nap. I've been really tired lately from school and studying, and it was good just to feel like I didn't have to do anything that I didn't want to do. I then walked back to the main trail and scouted out some places to maybe deer hunt this fall.

That evening, I had a freeze-dried chicken and rice dinner, then went inside my tent and read about Huck and Jim until I finished the book. It was almost dark by then, anyway. I slept really great, falling asleep to the sounds of the brook and whip-poor-wills.

The next morning, after breakfast, I packed up and headed for home. It was one of the best weekends of my life. Too bad I missed prom... yeah, right.

CHAPTER FORTY-SIX

ELLY

It felt weird that I went to prom as a freshman and sophomore, and wouldn't go to my junior-year one. On the other hand, I had all these mixed emotions on whether I wanted to go or not. My dating life has been a mess the whole time I've been in high school. I've gone out with the wrong kind of guy the whole time. Maybe I should just take a break from the whole dating scene—sort things out.

The problem is that now, I know what kind of boy would make me happy—a boy like Luke. Yet, that's the guy I've turned down twice this year when he's asked me out. I'm afraid I've blown it with him for good. We're still working together closely in Yearbook, but he's not teasing me like he usually does—he's just been business-like with me… friendly enough, but distant at the same time. I want to tell him I'm sorry, how wonderful he is, but there's something holding me back. Mom always told me, "Let the boy make the first move." But what if a guy already has made the first move and the second move, and the girl has rejected him? And she realizes now that she's been stupid. What does the instruction booklet say about that situation?

Two weeks before prom, Will, a senior in my Spanish class who I barely know, asked me out to prom. He seems nice, good-looking, and smart enough; but I hesitated to say yes when he asked me. Finally, I came up with a lame response. "Let me see if my mom thinks I'll have time to shop for a dress and get everything ready. Can I get back to you?"

The response got me out of an awkward situation, but it wasn't really fair to Will. As a senior, he obviously wanted to go to prom, and he probably had been working up his nerve to ask me for several days. If I said no after a few days of debating whether to go with him or not, it would make him have that much harder of a time to find a date.

After I got home from school that day, I asked Mom if we had enough time to get ready for prom, and she practically shrieked, "Yes! Let's go shopping this afternoon! Who's the boy? Who are his parents? Do I know them?" So I texted Will and said I would go with him, and would hopefully pick out a dress that evening.

When I had time to think back about Mom's reaction, it was so typical of her... the "who are his parents" thing. That seems so important to her, the status of a guy's parents. Suppose I had said Luke had asked me out, a guy whose parents are both dead and his dad had a record and died drunk-driving. I can just picture how she would have reacted to that.

Immediately after dinner, Mom and I left to go shopping. She was a lot more enthusiastic about the whole thing than I was, and she seemed clueless that I was so "uninspired." Finally, after over an hour of trying on various dresses, I selected a pinkish, coral-looking strapless dress. It had a design with jewels all over the top and a plain long bottom. It was a really, really nice dress, but it fit really tight and was very expensive. It just seemed like a waste of money to buy something that I was probably going to wear only one time to go out with a guy I barely know.

In the two weeks before prom, I didn't watch what I ate; and the dress was really, really tight by Saturday. I'm through agonizing over every time I gain or lose a pound or two. I'm not going down that road again for any guy. On Friday, the day before prom, I left school early and got my nails done. I always get acrylic nails for formal dances; those nails do look great even though they're so fake. Later on, I went and got a spray tan. No girl wants to be pale for prom. That stuff can't be good for my skin, though. But about every girl I know gets a spray tan for prom and homecoming.

On Saturday morning, I took a shower to wash off the excess of my spray tan. I then left to go to my 10:30 hair appointment. Mom and I decided to do an updo. The hair stylist pinned all of my hair up in a low bun, and added a braid when I said I wanted one. I asked for curls on both sides of my face, too. In all, I probably had 70 bobby pins and hairpins keeping my hair in place. After my hair appointment, Mom and I grabbed a quick bite to eat, then went to a florist to pick up the boutonniere for Will.

Next, we went to a beautician shop for this woman who Mom knows to do my makeup. When the woman was finished, the makeup was not good at all. Mom and I were both not satisfied. We went home and redid my entire face. Talk about a chaotic mess. I was stressed the whole time that we wouldn't finish before Will came.

A couple hours later, Will picked me up and he gave me my corsage. We went out to dinner instead of having dinner at prom. It was nice enough. We complained about Spanish class some, and he talked about getting ready for college. He's going to the university to major in… I've forgotten already.

We then went to prom; and it was nice enough, too. Caleb was there with Mary—well, now, that is a match made in heaven… two of a kind there—a loser abuser with a tramp and a gossip. Will and I danced some, sat some in awkward silences, and then he took me home and gave me the required kiss. No night of magic for me.

CHAPTER FORTY-SEVEN

MARCUS

I was really excited about going to prom with Camila. We went out twice before the dance, and I really enjoyed doing stuff with her. When we were dating the first time, I was all about taking her out to some fancy restaurant and impressing her. But this time, I wanted to talk to her and get to know her better. She is amazing to be around. I never realized that before.

For our first date, we actually sat down and threw out suggestions to each other about what we could go do. Finally, she came up with the idea of going on a hike in the national forest and having a picnic. I'd never done anything outdoorsy before, so I had to ask Luke in English class about where to go. He told me about this great one-mile hike on a trail that led to a waterfall. He said Camila and I could eat a picnic lunch at the waterfall. That was a great suggestion. We had a great time, plus it didn't cost anything, either.

For our second date, Camila and I went to see a play at the university. We got to talk a lot on the way up there. We stopped for a bite to eat before going to the play. Watching actors perform in person was way better than watching a movie. She's thinking of going there, too, but she hasn't decided for sure. I even saw one of the guys on the basketball team there, and he remembered me... which made me feel really good. He's a freshman, so I will be playing with him in less than 18 months. That's hard to believe. I know I'll just be a walk-on. Still, I'll be part of a D-1 team. Camila and I talked all the way home about what we had seen and what the university was like. I really hope she decides to go there.

Prom night at the local hotel was great. Camila and I came for the 6:30 dinner with Tuscan Breast of Chicken, Crab Mac and Cheese, and Braised Beef Short Rib as the entrees; plus mashed potatoes, vegetables, and a couple kinds of salads. There was this Ice Cream Sundae Buffet for dessert. Dancing with Camila was awesome. Obviously, the slow dances were special, with me holding her tight. One time, we gave each other a long kiss.

From 9:00 to 10:00, there were all these neat photo booths. My favorite one was where there were these cardboard limos, and you could get in one of them and pretend that you were on the way to somewhere special with your date and get pictures taken. Mr. Wayne was there with his wife, so I asked him if the two of them would get in the "front seat" of the limo, as if they were chauffeuring Camila and me to prom. Wayne laughed at that and said they would be glad to. So, Camila and I now have a photo of us being driven to prom by Mr. Wayne and his wife.

At 10:00, there was the Senior Lineup. All the seniors and their dates marched through and were announced. I thought it was kind of silly; but then I started thinking that at this time a year from now, Camila and I could be getting announced. And we would have barely over a month before not only the school year ended, but our high school careers ended. That's just crazy to think about.

I remember when I was a freshman, and it was the first period of my first day of high school, and I was in Ms. Hawk's English 9 Honors class. She was emphasizing how important it was to get off to a good start; that ninth-grade grades counted as much as senior grades; and before we knew it, our high school years would be over. She said that five years ago, she was sitting in her high school senior English class; and now, she was teaching a high school English class. Ms. Hawk said the time had gone by just like that, and she snapped her fingers.

I told Camila about what I was thinking, and she remembered that day in Ms. Hawk's class, too. Then she said she had been thinking about how fast the first three years of high school had gone when she was watching the Senior Lineup, and we were both really amazed that we had been thinking about the same thing.

"Are you worried, maybe scared, about the future?" Camila asked.

"I wasn't until just now," I said, and we both laughed.

But she added, "It is scary to think we're almost adults and a little over a year from now, we'll be living in a college dorm somewhere and be responsible for making good decisions, and our parents won't be around to tell us what to do or help us out."

It was pretty heavy stuff for a prom date, but that's another reason why I really like her. We just sat down and talked some more about life while almost everybody else was dancing. At 11:00, prom was over; and it was time for everybody, if they wanted, to go to the school for after-prom to play games, eat, talk, and just chill. We went to the school but didn't play any of the games or eat anything. We just sat and talked for an hour about our futures after our schooling was over. I swear, it was one of the best nights of my life.

CHAPTER FORTY-EIGHT

MIA

With money being so tight, I never expected to be going to prom during my high school years. Yet, even on the morning before prom, I forced myself to get up at 6 to start doing school work. Most of every Saturday and Sunday, I try to catch up on my reading and studying that I didn't get to do during the week. If I work really hard all weekend, I'm usually mostly caught up by late Sunday afternoon and can finally feel free to relax a little, maybe do something with my sisters or go for a walk. I worry about never getting any exercise or doing anything but school work.

But what usually happens after supper on Sunday is that I fall asleep around 7:00 and end up sleeping until 5:00 or so in the morning. Then I start feeling guilty all over again, and end up getting up and working on some college project or paper until it's time to go to class. So after breakfast on Saturday morning, I studied and did school work straight through to lunch. After lunch, Mama told me she was going to do my long, black hair in braids and also do my nails—that that was going to be her gift to me for prom. I already had felt bad about her making my prom dress, so her saying that just made me feel guiltier.

It was nice, though, sitting down with her and talking. And we did talk—a lot. I asked her how she was holding up; and

Mama said she was fine, that she had hired a lawyer to handle the divorce, that my father was living with Ann and was still working only a couple of days a week at his construction job. Mama said she had enrolled at the community college to take some more nursing classes beginning in the summer, and she was really looking forward to that. "We'll have more money after I finish up, too," she said and smiled.

Next, the conversation turned really heavy when I asked the questions I had been wanting to ask her for the longest time. "How do people fall out of love? How did the two of you fall out of love? I used to think that the two of you had true love. But I watched your marriage fall apart. Why?"

Mama thought for a long time, and finally said, "Sometimes, people fall out of love because both people change over time, or one person doesn't change while the other person grows. I think with your father and me, it was the second one. He just never changed in the way he thought about things. He never wanted to grow as a person. He never wanted to better himself in his jobs. He was still the teenage boy who swept me off my feet when we were in high school. I just didn't want to be married to a teenage boy anymore. Maybe it was that simple."

Mama then confided to me that she was worried about going through the whole dating thing again, and that no man would find her interesting or attractive. I assured her that she was still beautiful, that all kinds of men would find a pretty woman in her 30s like her attractive, and that men would be impressed with a woman trying to get more education.

"Thank you for saying that," she said. "Enough about me. Have you got a read on this Mateo yet?"

"I like him," I said. "He's really smart and good-looking."

"Is there a *but* in there anywhere?" she asked. "As in, 'but he's not Luke'?"

"I don't know," I replied. I told her that Luke and I had met once to talk after school, and I couldn't figure out how he felt about us, and that we had talked about getting together at some point to talk some more, but we hadn't... mostly because we had both been so busy with school.

"You should go after what you want in life, both for a man and a career," she said.

I was shocked when she said that. I replied, "I thought you always told me not to be forward around men, to let them make the first move."

"That advice was from a woman who is now in the process of getting divorced," she said. "So, you can now take that advice with a grain of salt. Now, enough of the serious talk. I've got some ideas on how we should do your makeup."

I admit that it was nice for Mama to fuss over me all afternoon and to watch my sisters watching us. Were they thinking that one day, they would be going to a prom with a handsome guy? And I admit that it was nice being picked up by Mateo and taken to a glitzy, historic hotel with chandeliers and a high ceiling painted to show the constellations.

I needed someone to tell me how great I looked, to open the car door for me, to hold my hand as we strolled into the room. Mateo and I sat at a table with Marcus and Camila, Elly and Will, and Allen and Paige. It was nice to have Elly, Paige, and Camila tell me how great I looked when we went to the restroom to freshen up. They had never met Mateo before, and the three of them were raving about how good-looking he was and how attentive to me he was.

But the truth was that after dinner, when Mateo and I were either dancing or sitting and talking, we ran out of things to talk about. We exhausted the subject of our college classes early in the evening; and for most of the rest of the night, the conversation was mostly on how great everybody looked and what a great time we were having.

When prom was over at 11:00, I said I was too worn out from school to go to after-prom, which was the truth. But I was also bored and wanted to get a couple of hours of sleep before working all day Sunday on homework. I needed at least five hours of sleep before hitting the books.

STATE TESTING

CHAPTER FORTY-NINE

LUKE

I knew Tuesday was going to be bad, with the essay part of the English state test in the morning and the Chemistry one in the afternoon. But I had no idea how bad it would be.

Things started to fall apart on Monday. Miss Roche was a nervous wreck in English class, making us do another one of those ridiculous writing prompts. This time, the topic was "What is more important—nature or nurture?" It made me think of Dad and how I hoped I would never be like him genetically with the alcoholism and all that junk, and would never treat my kids like he did me.

I got so depressed and angry about him that I hadn't even started on the prompt when Miss Roche began "checking for understanding." She was angry when she saw that I hadn't written anything down, and wanted to know what I had been doing instead of the prompt. I wanted to say, "thinking about my dead father and whether I'm like him or not." But the poor woman was so agitated anyway, I just mumbled, "having trouble getting started." That sent her off on another loud sermon about how we needed "to be focused tomorrow."

Our English class is really smart, and she's a really good teacher. Nobody is going to fail the English state test. But I bet she's worried that somebody might, and how bad having failures in an honors class would make her look. So I guess I can cut her some slack for being in full-blown teacher-panic mode.

Chemistry class review was even worse. Mrs. Wilson seemed even more stressed out than Ms. Roche was, if that was even possible. Class was one long blur of acids, bases, chemical bonds and reactions and, of course, everybody's favorite—the periodic table. Throw in a little thermochemistry and electrochemistry, and my head felt like ice picks had been stabbed into it. Before the review, I was worried about failing the test. After the review, I was sure I was screwed and summer school-bound.

When I got home, I got a real scare. I found Granddaddy sitting on the floor with a knot on his head and his right hand bleeding. He couldn't tell me what had happened, but there was a broken glass on the floor. I guess that's how he cut himself. The gash was pretty deep, so I called the hospital; and the nurse told me to take him to the emergency room.

We sat in there for close to an hour in the "emergency" room before some nurse came to get us. It was agony sitting in that place for so long, feeling helpless and not being able to help the person in my family who has always meant the most to me. Finally, this doctor patched Granddaddy up, all the while asking him a bunch of questions that Granddaddy couldn't answer. Then the doctor left him with the nurse to finish things up, and told me to come with him.

The doctor wanted to know how long Granddaddy had "been like this," and who his personal physician was. After a while, the doctor finally got to the point and said, "Your grandfather may be suffering from the early stages of dementia. Is it just the two of you?"

I had been trying to talk myself out of the possibility that Granddaddy was starting to lose it. Maybe I should've gone to a doctor earlier. I told the doctor that my parents were dead and Granddaddy was divorced, and that it was just us. I also told him I didn't know what to do or who to call. He told me he nurse would help set me up with a doctor to call, and said that Granddaddy probably shouldn't be driving anymore.

When we got home, it was too late to call for a doctor's appointment. But I figured I could go to the main office on Tuesday between the English and Chemistry state tests, and make an appointment. I had a rough night, tossing and turning, worrying about Granddaddy most of the time and the Chemistry test and all the rest. I wasn't worried about the English test. If there's one thing in school I'm good at, it's writing.

One of the things that Miss Roche had hammered into us on Monday was to have fully charged laptops to take the test. Partway through the second semester, the school system got a grant to get laptops for everybody, and one of the conditions was that we had to use them for the state tests. But the strangest thing happened when we got to the library for the test. Me and only two other people had remembered to either charge or bring their laptops. The state doesn't allow teachers to give their own state tests, so we had another English teacher, Ms. Barnes, as our test proctor. Ms. Barnes was in a real panic about most of the students not having their laptops, as she had to get the library's PCs set up in a hurry.

Halfway through answering the writing prompt, my laptop mysteriously turned itself off. It was my turn to panic. Miss Barnes had to send for Mrs. Roberts, who was also the state test coordinator for the school. I could tell by the way Roberts looked at me that she thought the whole laptop malfunction thing was my fault. Next came this long debate between Barnes and Roberts over whether time should be spent fixing the laptop or sending me to a PC. Did that mean I would have to start the writing prompt over? Would that make me late for the Chemistry state test? When would I have time to call the doctor about Granddaddy? No lunch for me today… I'd have to take the Chemistry state test on an empty stomach. Oh, happy day.

Roberts finally figured out how to get my laptop going again. But by then, I had totally lost my train of thought; and had to go back and read my essay from the start. I was the last person to finish the prompt and didn't have time to eat lunch. When I went to the office to call the doctor's office, I was put on hold for a really long time and kept getting shuffled off to extension this and extension that. Then it took forever to set up a time with the appointment person because I had to try to get an after-school appointment, which is hard to get because that's when just about everybody wants one.

I was so stressed from Monday's disasters, the laptop falling apart, and being hungry that the Chemistry test was a catastrophe from the start. I knew it before I got a third of the way through; my mind just couldn't focus.

A week later, the scores came back. Miss Roche said she was really happy with me, that I had scored in the top five percent on the writing test. Not bad for a boy who didn't do a single comma worksheet for homework all year. I made a 305 on the Chemistry thing, *only* 95 points below passing… not even good enough for *expedited* retakes.

"Which would you prefer, before- or after-school remediation?" said Mrs. Wilson when she *discreetly* called me up to her desk. That's like deciding between death by poison or death by strangulation.

CHAPTER FIFTY

ELLY

It was Paige who came up with the idea, and it was brilliant. On Monday, during lunch, Paige, Camila, Kylee, Hannah, and I were sitting around, complaining about what a rough day Tuesday was going to be with the English state writing test in the morning and the Chemistry one in the afternoon. None of us were worried about failing either one of the state tests. All of us have an *A* in both classes, but we know the writing prompt is going to take a long time to do, and everything that has to do with Chemistry is time-consuming.

Really, the only fear we had about taking the tests was spending all those hours taking them on those laptops the school handed out a month or so ago. They're so cheap, and the keys are so small that they're a real pain to type on. Plus, they're always breaking down. They're not nearly as nice as the ones my parents bought for my brothers and me to take to school. Yet, the students have to use the stupid school laptops. And they suck up power so badly that they seem like they're always having to be recharged. Almost everybody hates them. I can't see why we can't take the state tests on the library's PCs like we used to.

So Paige said, "Why don't the four of us text everybody in English class and tell them to leave their laptops at home? Then when we go to take the writing test, some of us can say we forgot to charge them, and some of us can say we forgot and left them at home. And some of us can say that our laptops weren't working that morning for some reason."

After Paige said that, we were all about that plan. By the end of lunch, the four of us had texted everybody in class except Luke, who doesn't have a cell phone. I told everyone I would tell him in Yearbook. Well, we texted everybody except Luke because of the phone thing; and except Caleb and Mary, who nobody likes. Personally, I wouldn't have minded if both their laptops had broken down during the test. Everybody we texted was down with the plan.

The next day, Ms. Barnes, one of the other English teachers, brought us into the library; and only Luke, Caleb, and Mary had their laptops. I felt so bad for Luke. In Yearbook, I had forgotten to tell him not to bring his. Something was bothering him all period when we were working together. I kept worrying that he was maybe upset about me breaking our date last month. I still feel so bad about that, I just forgot to tell him what everybody decided about the laptops.

By the time Ms. Barnes had checked in five of the students and given them their test tickets, she knew something was up. I mean, five students gave the same excuses about not having their laptops. She threw a fit and had to go set up the PCs in the other part of the library. She's got a reputation as a good teacher, and I'll probably have her for senior English. It's not her fault those laptops suck. I felt bad that we pulled that stunt on her—but not too bad, if you know what I mean.

After Ms. Barnes had moved everybody to the other side of the library, she was so frustrated that she got confused on the directions and read the wrong ones from the test manual. We ended up being 45 minutes late in starting the test; but once we got underway, it was a breeze working on a PC. About 30 minutes after the test started, Luke's laptop broke down, and then Mary's just a minute or two later did... which sent Miss Barnes into panic mode again. I felt really, really bad for her then, and I felt even worse for Luke. He'd looked really depressed on Monday, and he looked worse on Tuesday. The poor guy was still there working on his essay when the rest of us went to lunch.

On Wednesday in Yearbook, I told him I had forgotten to tell him about the laptop plot; and I said I felt really bad about it, considering what he had gone through during the state test. He said he had been so out of it that he hadn't even thought about why so many people were having laptop problems.

I said, "Can I help with anything? Do you want to talk?" What I wanted to say was, "Would you like to get together this weekend and do something?" I wanted to say that really badly, but couldn't quite get the words out.

Then Luke said, "The doctor thinks Granddaddy has dementia. I've been noticing that he isn't right. He also seems a lot weaker than he used to. I don't know what I'm going to do. I feel guilty about leaving him alone in the house by himself. But I'd feel guilty about missing school to stay with him."

"Why don't you go to Mrs. Whitney?" I said. "Maybe she can help tell you what to do. Maybe she could tell you how to get one of those home health care workers to come over and be with him during the day."

"That's a great idea," Luke said, and I smiled when I saw his face brighten up. Then he turned sad-looking again and said, "Elly, I know I failed the Chemistry state test. As soon as the scores come back, I know I'm screwed."

"I bet you didn't fail, Luke," I said. "You're too hard on yourself." Then, I thought he probably did fail; he's just awful in math and anything that has to do with figures. Next, I remembered how Mia used to tutor him, and I thought maybe I should offer to help him out. But if I did that, it would seem like I thought he had already failed. So I ended up doing nothing and being indecisive. Why can't I ever make the right decisions with this boy—the sweetest one in the whole school, and probably the best one for me?

A few days later, the Chemistry scores came back. Sure enough, Luke told me he had failed and was getting tutored in the mornings before school. I should have offered earlier to help him out.

CHAPTER FIFTY-ONE

MARCUS

That "shaky *B*" in Honors Chemistry has changed into a "shaky *C*." No matter how much I study or how many hours I spend at night working on that stupid crap, nothing helps. A week before the state test on the class, I was complaining to Camila about how much I was struggling. She did the nicest thing: she offered to get together and tutor me one night.

I asked Mom if I could have Camila over to tutor me, and she just went nuts with both joy and questions. She's been wanting to meet Camila, anyway. Mom really liked Kylee and got to be around her four or five times when we were dating. Mom and Dad used to have a lot to say about my immaturity and school... especially girl-related issues. But one thing they have never complained about is the girls I've brought over to our house.

Camila came over the Friday before the test. We decided our date for the weekend would be her coming over for dinner. After she tutored me for a couple of hours, we could go and binge-watch some show on Netflix until it was time for her to go home. Mom and Camila hit it off right away. Camila had told me to tell Mom that she would bring some traditional Dominican dessert, and Mom was really impressed that Camila knew about her heritage and wanted to share it. What she brought (and I think I got the name right) was something called *Pudín de Pan*, some sort of zesty bread pudding. Both Mom and Dad raved about how good it was, and they were right.

During dinner, I got a little irritated with Mom when she started asking all these questions about Camila's favorite classes and college plans. But I guess that is what moms are supposed to do. She couldn't compliment Camila's outfit all dinner long; and the weather topic was exhausted pretty quick, too.

After dinner was over, we went downstairs to study. One of the things I like best about Camila is that she comes straight to the point about everything. She said, "What worries you most about the state test? Tell me, and we'll hit it hard."

"That's easy," I said. "Acid-base chemistry and equilibria."

"Great, that's one of my strong points," she said, which just amazed me. We spent about an hour going over formulas and how to break them down so that they could be understood better. After about 15 minutes of her tutoring, I actually began to understand the stuff better.

Next, I said I needed some help (well, a lot of help) on ionic and covalent bonds, and she even helped me get comfortable with that stuff. We worked for almost three hours, reviewing what we had been covering in class. I felt so much better after we finished than I did before.

"You are freaking awesome," I said when we finished.

"I know," she said right back. "It's good that you realize that." She laughed when she said the second part, like she was teasing. But the truth is that Camila is a really impressive girl... I should say woman. No wonder she didn't like me bossing her around when we dated in the ninth grade. I'm glad she gave me a second chance. I really do hope she decides to go to the university. I would really like to still be dating her then.

Next, we talked about the plot that she and her girlfriends cooked up about everybody leaving their laptops at home for the English state test. I was really glad when she texted me about that. Those school laptops are pathetic. My fingers are too big for those tiny little keys, and I'm constantly hitting the wrong letter.

We had studied for so long, and it was so exhausting that neither one of us felt like watching TV. So, she said she had better head home. I asked her how I could repay her; and once again, she came straight to the point. "A kiss for now, and a promise to take me out to dinner for when, not if, you pass the state test."

I was obviously down with that, especially the first part. When the testing day finally came, the Chemistry test was hard, but I didn't feel overwhelmed. I took my time like Camila had told me to; and I went through, like, three pages of scrap paper that Mrs. Wilson handed out for us to work on. The scores came back a week later. I made a 438, well above the 400 I needed. Mom and Dad were really pleased with me, and Mom kept raving about Camila.

She and I went out to dinner, as she promised we would. We both decided to order lobster, but it was worth the cost. The meal was perfect; being with her was perfect. I feel like all this stress has been lifted off me. I'll probably have an *A* on everything else for the year; and maybe now, I can bring the Honors Chemistry grade up to a *B*. I'm going to a university to play basketball, I've got a great girlfriend, and the hardest year of high school is just about over. I don't see how things could be much better for me right now.

CHAPTER FIFTY-TWO

MIA

All the emphasis that the school and teachers place on these state tests is absolutely ridiculous. I get that the tests are how an individual school and a school system are ranked. I get that these tests determine whether or not the state will punish a school, and maybe even take away its certification. But the tests and all that preparation are lame: the non-stop drilling on simple things... all that practice on how to take a test. The tests themselves, except for the English writing component, are all multiple-guess.

Yeah, you heard me right—the tests are multiple-guess, not multiple-choice. The teachers waste hours teaching us to make good guesses (what they mean are lucky guesses) on the test. A state test's basic premise is that there are four possible answers for each question. One answer is so stupid that almost nobody would choose it. A second one sounds like it could be right, but it really has nothing to do with the real answer. And the last two answers are vague and poorly written, and both seem to be right. But there's some little clue in one of the answers that makes it the right one.

Now, really, how pathetic is that as a way to judge whether a student is "proficient" in a subject? If those mysterious "powers that be" really wanted to judge a student's competency in a subject, there would be tons of short-answer questions.

There would be a major essay to write where a student would have to write about some essential point that had to be learned for the class. But then the state testing companies would have to spend a lot of money hiring really knowledgeable people to grade the things. No, we can't have that because it would probably cut into the obscene profits they make.

I've done some research on this topic. The whole testing thing is a scam. Not only is the taking of the tests and the drilling for the tests wasting my time, but it also takes up all this class time when the teacher could actually be teaching something that would help us in college. I get so bored when we are test-drilling. I'm sick of it. I've got to get ready for college. Drilling on how to take multiple-guess tests is not helping to prepare me for college or life afterward. Name one time in the real world when I'm going to have to take a multiple-guess test.

On Monday afternoon, before the state test on Tuesday, I was in Miss Roche's English 11 A.P. class. She said we had to answer a writing prompt in preparation for the English state writing test the next day. The night before, I had studied till midnight, gotten up at 5:30 like I almost always do, gulped down a bowl of cereal, and studied for two hours before heading to the community college. I sat through college lectures all morning and had been through state test prepping all afternoon in my other high school classes. I was in no mood to write a ridiculous writing prompt for a subject that I have a 100 average in; for a state test that I will, without a doubt, make a perfect score on, or close to a perfect score. I had the usual five or six hours of homework staring me in the face, so I decided to get out my BIO 142 textbook and start working on the professor's assignment.

I had never disobeyed a teacher's instructions the whole time I've been in school, but I had just had enough. I know I'm on track to be my class' valedictorian. I know a lot of students at this school look up to me. I am really, really honored by that. I want to be a role model. But I was just fed up.

Miss Roche was coming around the room, checking on how we were doing. When she came to my desk and saw a college biology book open and me working on homework, there was like this look of horror and disbelief. She said, "Mia, I'm shocked that you're not doing what I asked you all to do. Can you explain yourself?"

"Miss Roche," I said very politely and slowly. "Are you really worried about *me* failing the English writing prompt? Are you really worried about *anyone* in here failing the writing prompt? I'm not meaning to be disrespectful to you in any way. I'm just all stressed out over the time it takes to do this college work. I'm just trying to knock some of it out now so I won't have to spend past midnight tonight working on it."

After I said that, I felt like everybody in the class was looking at me. And I looked up; and sure enough, all the kids were staring at Miss Roche and me. The poor woman was still speechless after what I had said.

After this long pause, she finally said something. "Mia, I understand where you're coming from. It's just that the school tells us that we have to spend time reviewing for the state test."

She paused for a little while, then continued. "I know none of you are going to have trouble with the prompt. I know all of you are going to score really high on the essay."

Then Donovan, one of the smartest guys in the school and who is taking classes at the community college like everybody else in the room, said, "Why don't you pretend that we're working on the writing prompt? All of us can then get out our college assignments and work on them. We can get some of our work done and won't have to spend so much time on it tonight. Maybe we can get some sleep for a change, and be better prepared for the state test."

It was a brilliant idea, and I was so hoping that Miss Roche would go for it. And she did! "Yes, just work on your writing prompts, folks," she said. "Come up to my desk if you're having any problems. And if you're not coming up to my desk, I will *assume* that you're done with the writing prompt. And you can *assume* that I'm not up here grading papers from fifth period."

With that, she sat down and started grading papers from some other class. I got my bio work done. That night, I was able to go to bed really early—around 11:00. And when the writing scores came back, everybody in class had aced it... just like all of us—and Miss Roche—knew we would. Miss Roche is a really cool teacher.

SUMMER JOBS

CHAPTER FIFTY-THREE

LUKE

Well, on my third try, I passed the Chemistry state test. I made a 385 the second time around, which qualified me for the wonderful, expedited retake phase of "the stupid person who can't pass tests the first two times" contest. Stand up and cheer, please. I made an *impressive* 405 on the Chemistry test that third time, and was pronounced "proficient" in the crap. I hope it's the last ever Chemistry test I'll ever take in my life. As much as I love Biology, I had thought a little about being a science major in college. But that idea is over now. It looks like it's gonna be English, maybe with a minor in History.

There are only two weeks left in the school year, the state tests are over, and it's like this giant stress balloon has been popped. You've either passed or failed a class by now, and your grades are pretty much locked in place. I've clinched a *D* in Chemistry and in my remedial math class because my inability to do what for everybody else is "simple math" reared its ugly, stupid head. I can hardly wait for Algebra II next year. I'll be one of the few seniors taking that class. Just about everybody who's college-bound will be moving on to Trigonometry or Calculus. Gee, I'm real sorry I'm missing out on those two biggies. After I had marched down the aisle with my cap and gown on, I would be so looking forward to going to summer school for math.

I've been job-hunting after school for the last week or so—filling out applications, going for interviews, that sort of stuff. I thought about starting up my old lawn-mowing business, but I don't want to go back to those days. Besides, that old lawn mower I used then is barely able to finish mowing Granddaddy's and my lawn before coughing and spitting to a stop. We need a new lawn mower; but I also need to pay the electric bill, phone bill, grocery bill—it goes on and on—every month.

Granddaddy is no help with any of the bills. When I look at his checkbook, his handwriting is so poor, I can't figure out what it was he paid for. He can't remember anything anymore; and when I ask him what bill is coming up this month beyond the usual ones, he can't recall what bills come when. Thank goodness he paid off the house long ago. Thank goodness a Social Security check comes every month. It's been exhausting dealing with him and managing the house and all the bills. I would never have thought that taking care of just two people would be so hard. There's just not enough money coming in. That's why I've been looking so hard to find a job.

I finally found one on Tuesday. It's at a fast food joint downtown. I'm the new maintenance man. That's business-speak for janitor. You knew these companies save their best-paying, most emotionally rewarding, most self-satisfying jobs for seventeen-year-olds, didn't you?

Actually, I had the choice of mopping the floors, cleaning the toilets, washing the windows, hauling trash to the dumpster, picking up trash in the parking lot, and generally being as dirty as a pig every day after work... or... "manning a register." Me, with my math skills, trying to keep orders straight and figuring out what the daily specials were? Trying to make change and typing in the right numbers? I would have had math panic all day, every day.

So, I chose the janitor position since I had a choice, plus

the fact that it pays a whole dime more per hour—a dime above minimum wage. Obviously, and I say this with extreme pride, me being the sanitation engineer for a major American business will look great on any college application. "My," they will say in the admissions office, "that young prodigy has to be admitted to our school before Harvard snaps him up." I'm not in a real good mood right now, can you tell?

I started work on Wednesday, after school. The basic plan, the manager said, is I will work two or three hours after school and get as much "simple maintenance" done as possible. Then I can "catch up on weekends," when I will work nine-hour shifts. There goes my weekend fishing trips.

Once school lets out, I will work full nine-hour shifts Tuesday through Sunday, 5:00 A.M. to 2:00 P.M, with an hour's worth of breaks. I can get the place spiffed up some (that means cleaning the toilets) before the breakfast crowd comes in from 6:00 to 9:00. Then I can give the johns another good cleaning right before I clock out. In between cleaning the toilets, I can get everything else done.

The first evening I worked, I could tell the manager was testing me. It was like he was seeing how I would handle all the worst jobs before he took the time to fully train me. If I was going to quit, the man probably wanted me to do it within the first few days. Then he could hire somebody else before the super-busy summer season started.

I know that was what he was doing because I spent much of that first evening hauling trash bags to the dumpster and picking up all kinds of crap in the parking lot. There's nothing quite like the smell of chocolate milkshakes that have been marinating inside a trash bag for a day or two. It's almost as wonderful as the aroma from a toilet that's been stopped up since early in the morning. Good times, good times. I just hope I can save some of my money for college. As long as the pickup keeps chugging along, the mower keeps gasping along, the washing machine keeps churning around, and the house remains standing, I should be fine.

CHAPTER FIFTY-FOUR

ELLY

Mom and Dad have decided I need to find a summer job so I can develop some responsibility. In the past, they've always wanted me to keep my summers free for all those enrichment-type camps they send me to. And of course, during the school year, they've always said "school is your job."

Actually, I did really want to work this summer. I've never worked before—never really wanted to, which just shows how pampered I've been my whole life. I didn't even know how to start looking. I asked Dad for some tips on where to apply, and he suggested that our club would be a good place to start. He said the club has a summer recreation program where they would probably be needing people to play games with kids and read to them. Dad gave me the name of somebody to call. He also said to wait until he had called the club before I did.

When I did call, the man I talked to acted as if he knew I was going to call, and told me to come on in for an interview. I was really nervous about my first job interview, but the questions were more along the line of whether I would need to take much time off during the summer for family vacations. I think Dad must have arranged for me to get the job before I even called.

The pay is really good, from what Mia and Camila told

me. Any job that pays three dollars more per hour than minimum wage like this one does is fantastic, they said. At first, I was really excited about getting the job. But then the more I thought about it, probably the real reason why I got the job was because my family belongs to the club, and my dad knew the right person.

I went in this past Saturday morning for some training, and to get a taste of what I would be doing. Basically, my hours are 9:00 to 1:00, and I will spend my time as one of the assistants to the program director. I will be reading during story time; playing indoor games; and taking kids on nature walks around the grounds, where I will point out birds, tree species, and things like that. We'll also do what the program manager calls "creek stomps," where we'll take seines and capture minnows, crayfish, and these aquatic bugs and tell how they fit into the ecosystem.

I can tell what a minnow and crayfish is, but I've got no idea what to call all those aquatic bugs except, well, bugs. The only person I know who could identify them would be Luke, and then I got this brilliant idea. I told Luke about my summer job and how I would be leading creek stomps, and asked if he could help me learn some things.

He got really excited about that, so we made a "date" for Saturday after he got off work, and I had finished my training at the club. He told me to meet him at this entrance to the national forest, and we would walk a short distance to a creek and seine up creatures and identify them. On the way, he would point out trees to me and identify some bird songs.

When he showed up, he was still dressed in his fast food "uniform." He was filthy and sweaty. I guess he must have noticed how I was looking at him because he sarcastically said, "I'm the janitor there, making a whole dime more than minimum wage, so I'm raking in the dough. I do get a tad dirty, as you can probably tell."

As soon as we got inside the woods, Luke said, "Hear that Eastern wood pewee singing? It says its name over and over… pee-weeeee. That's how you learn bird songs. Learn them phonetically like that, or use some memory trick."

I listened for a little while, and Luke was right: the pewee was saying its name over and over. Then he said he heard an American redstart, which has a song like a squeaky bicycle wheel. I listened to the redstart singing for a little while, and then I felt like I could permanently identify it. The song really did sound like somebody riding a bicycle that needs oil.

I was so impressed by Luke and what he could do out in the woods that I said something that I was realize now was pretty hurtful. "You should have applied for my country club job. You'd have been perfect."

"Elly, there's no way they would have hired me, except as a busboy or dishwasher," he said, with just a touch of an edge to his voice. "I'm not their kind of person. Who you know is more important than what you know."

"I didn't mean…" I stammered, and he interrupted me.

"I know you didn't," he said. "I'm sorry I sort of snapped at you. I wouldn't hurt your feelings for all the world. Let's forget about it. I want to show you some blacknose dace down at the creek. They're really easy to identify, and that country club creek is bound to be full of them."

But I couldn't forget about it or forgive myself for what I said to him. He was right about what he said about the club not hiring him except for some menial job, even if he had applied. I got my job not because I was qualified for it, but because of who my parents are. And then another thought came to me: my parents would absolutely freak out if they knew I was alone with Luke out in the woods, especially Dad.

Yet there was really no one I could have been safer with in the woods, or who would have known what to do if we came across a venomous snake or a bear or something. He would have protected me. He was right, too, about him never hurting my feelings "for all the world." At that moment, I would have given anything in the world if he had taken my hand and held it while we walked down to the creek.

CHAPTER FIFTY-FIVE

MARCUS

For the last couple of weeks, my parents and I have been talking about what kind of job I should try to get for the summer. In the past, I've spent the summer lifting weights or doing running drills on my own before football practice started. Football practice always started well before the school year began, so my summers were always really short. But, of course, football has long been over for me.

It's kind of sad that I'll never again be running out onto the field with the other guys before a game starts. The National Anthem being played, me looking into the stands for Mom and Dad and whoever I was dating at the time, the coin flip, the starters being announced. The smells from the locker room, the smell of freshly cut grass out on the field, the kickoff. All those rituals and things that are such an important part of the game. I know I'll miss that. But it's time to move on.

To what, though, is the question. Especially during the summer, in early May, it suddenly occurred to me that I had the whole summer free. So that's when I first went to my parents about what kind of job they thought I should apply for. Dad said his business had summer internships available; but he felt that since it looks like I'm going to be a history major, maybe I should look for something in that area, which would "build my resume." Mom said that since she's a real estate agent, there's nothing available in her office that would be relevant to my future.

I ended up going to Mr. Wayne and asking him for help on what I should do. He said that I should call the local museum and see if they had anything available, although any position that was open would probably be a volunteer one. If that didn't work out, given my love for sports, maybe I could apply to be an usher at the local minor league ballpark. Or I could try to get a job refereeing summer basketball leagues. I decided to call the museum first and ended up talking to the assistant curator. She said that they always needed volunteers in the summer, but there were no paying jobs open.

She said one of the volunteer positions that was open was as a scribe. I would read and try to figure out what had been written down on these letters which had been sent home by local soldiers in World Wars I and II, Korea, and Vietnam. The museum had all these old letters that they had been meaning to decipher for years and years. The goal is to eventually put them in a tabletop-type book for sale at the museum. She said the working title was *Thoughts from the War Front to the Homefront.*

She said it would be tedious work at times, but it would give me real insight into what those soldiers were thinking about, how they were handling being in danger, and what their thoughts and feelings were toward their loved ones left at home. I was really excited about doing that, but I also knew I had to have some money. Mom and Dad have always given me all the money I've ever needed—even when they probably shouldn't have. But I think now, I want to earn some money that's mine and that I'm responsible for getting.

After I talked to the museum's assistant curator, I asked Dad what he thought about the volunteer job; and he said it would look great on a college resume. He also suggested that I call our club and see if there were any summer jobs there. Maybe I could combine the volunteer job and a real one.

With that thought, I called the club. The person I talked to put me through to the personnel guy for the place. He said that they needed someone to "hold down" the pool snack bar from noon to 5:00. The job doesn't pay all that well, just a dollar more per hour than minimum wage. But I could see how I could juggle volunteering at the museum and working at the pool snack bar.

The museum doesn't open to the public until 9:00, but the assistant curator says I could come in at 8:00 when she does and work until 10:00 or 10:30, then take a break and go onto my pool job. Luke has been encouraging me to run cross country with him next fall, saying that the team could use me... that it would help get me in great shape for basketball. I decided to go talk to Coach Henson about the cross country thing, and he agreed with Luke.

So my game plan for the summer is now to get up at 5:00, eat a light breakfast, and stretch. Then go running with Luke for three or four miles out on the highway somewhere or up into the national forest, go to the museum, then the pool, and be home for dinner around 5:30. I'll be working at the pool from Tuesday through Sunday of every week, and at the museum from Monday through Friday mornings. I'm not going to have a lot of free time, except in the evenings.

But Camila and I will have to time go out in the evenings some, and that will be awesome. And I'll have time to do my summer reading for English A.P. and Government, plus Mr. Wayne has suggested some books for me to read over the break. He said I should start reading a series called *The Saxon Stories* by Bernard Cornwell. It's all about what was going on in Britain in the ninth and tenth centuries—sounds kind of interesting because those people were really brutal to each other. I think this is going to be a really good summer... definitely different from what I've done in the past.

CHAPTER FIFTY-SIX

MIA

I've been so busy and stressed with school that it didn't dawn on me until recently that I needed a summer job. Mrs. Whitney had already suggested that I take a class at the community college over the summer to ease the burden a little in my senior year. I could use "some easing of the burden."

So I went to my college advisor, Dr. Myers, and she suggested that I take Chemistry 111 over the summer. She said it would be exploring the fundamental laws, theories, and mathematical concepts of chemistry. It shouldn't be too hard for me. There would be the usual three hours of lectures and three hours of lab during the week. But the best thing from my point of view was that all the class and lab time would be first thing every morning.

I told Dr. Meyers that after I finished up the college class every day, I could go to work somewhere. Then she said the nicest thing. "Have you thought about applying here to be a lab assistant? Maybe even do some tutoring in our entry-level summer biology classes?" I said I hadn't, and she offered to help me apply. Just like that, she dialed somebody, a Dr. Garnett who is in charge of the college's science department, and arranged for me to get an interview that very day after A.P. English at high school was over.

I hadn't talked to Dr. Garnett but for around 15 minutes, and she offered me a job with really good pay. I'll be an aide in the labs everyday between 10:00 and 3:00, and also assisting Dr. Garnett in her summer school introductory-level biology class for incoming freshmen. I'll work with the kids who struggled with high school biology and science classes, and are likely to do the same in college. I think it will really be satisfying to help students who are trying to do well but just can't seem to get the hang of something. When I used to tutor Luke in math, I always found that rewarding.

All this was really encouraging. But then I realized that I still needed more money for college, and to help out Mama. So, I started thinking of what kind of job I could get that would pay pretty well, and I could work in the evening. The one that popped into my head was waitressing, which Camila had told me she had been hired to do. She's already started working two nights a week, and she said the "tips are fantastic."

Later, Camila told me who to call at her restaurant, and I got an interview with the owner for the next day after school. Maybe the man was impressed with me during the interview, or maybe he was just desperate to get somebody started as soon as possible. He hired me right on the spot. Once school is over, I'll be working at the restaurant from 4:00 to 9:00 every evening from Tuesday through Sunday. So the only times this summer when I won't be in class, tutoring, or waitressing will be on weekend mornings and Monday nights. I guess that's when I'll have to do most of my studying and reading for Chem 111. But my life has to be like this—stressful and overscheduled—for now if I want to accomplish my goals and dreams. If I got through this past school year still standing, I can handle just about anything. I survived my parents' breakup, studying and going to school for 18 or 19 hours a day, going without hardly any sleep, and not having hardly any normal human relationships. I guess I can get through this.

Actually, things have settled down a little with just two weeks left in the school year; make that settled down a lot. The college classes are over now, and I made my usual *A* in everything. But that's hardly worth saying. For the first time in my academic career, I was really challenged, and I was ready for it.

We're not doing hardly anything in my high school classes now. It's like the school lets out this collective sigh of relief when those state tests are through. Camila came to me the other day and said the restaurant owner had asked her to now work three nights a week. She had said yes since school was winding down. She added that she could ask the manager if he needed me to come in and get training, and I said yes because I could use the money.

So, on Friday of last week, I spent my first night as a waitress as an assistant to this older woman named Amanda who has been there for a long time. I thought the job was going to be really easy; but it didn't take long to see that there's stress in that, too. Just about everybody wants to modify every little thing on the menu. Still, most of the evening went pretty well; but we had two customers, both men, who were real jerks.

The first man ordered a medium-rare steak of some kind, then complained when Amanda and I brought out his meal, saying that the steak was obviously overcooked. He said that before he even cut into it. Then he finally sliced it and complained some more, and said his baked potato wasn't hot enough, either. There was nothing wrong with the steak or potato, but Amanda had to act subservient to the jerk and bring him another meal. After going through all that with the man, the tip he left was pathetic.

The other incident occurred late in the evening, when Amanda was overwhelmed and asked me to go around and ask her customers if they needed any more water, lemon slices, or anything. These two guys who must have been in their 40s were eating alone, and asked me what time I got off work and if I had any plans for the evening. I said I had to work really late, and my boyfriend was picking me up. It was a pretty good spur-of-the-moment lie, and seemed to satisfy them. Their tip wasn't any good, either.

THE FUTURE

CHAPTER FIFTY-SEVEN

LUKE

It's the last day of school, and I don't know why I even bothered to come. I'm sitting in Miss Roche's first-period English 11 A.P class, which has 22 students in it; and only 10 of us are here. Frankly, I'm surprised it's that many. Miss Roche asked if we wanted to watch a movie, but most kids just sort of shrugged and said they wanted to play video games on their phones. Miss Roche looked like she was doing end-of-the-year reports or something.

I'm feeling indifferent to the whole "end of the school year" thing. Tomorrow, I become a full-time janitor for the next 10 weeks, so that's not much of a vacation. Better than school? I probably won't think so when I'm taking trash to the dumpster or cleaning toilets.

It's been a long, hard school year. Everybody said that junior year was going to be the worst year of high school—they had that right. But right now, I'm thinking about my future… my post-janitor, post-high school life. More than ever, I know what I want, and I know the order in which I want them.

First, I want a really good wife. I did a lot of dating this year... well, a lot more than I thought I would… enough dating to really think hard about the type of girl I want to spend the rest of my life with. None of the girls I dated in my junior year measured up to Mia, who I spent so much time with when we were freshman and who I dated my entire sophomore year. She is the complete package: a good and kind person, great personality, intelligent, beautiful, and someone who would make a great mother and partner.

The best person I dated all year was Leigh. She's a good person, she's smart, she's fun to be with; but she's not in Mia's league, not by a long shot. The only girl at this school who would be is Elly. Right now, she's sitting across the room and talking with Paige and Kylee, and I would give anything to have her sitting next to me and talking to me about what we wanted to do during the summer. Elly is really special.

But I asked her out twice during the school year, and I'm not going to ask her out a third time. One, it would be humiliating; and two, I don't think I could stand it for her to turn me down again. The other day, I was so glad that she asked me to help her learn how to identify some plants and animals for her summer job. Spending time with her this year when we were covering games for Yearbook or doing Yearbook spreads was literally the high point of my year.

When we were walking through the woods together that Saturday, I wanted to stop, hold her hand, and tell her how I felt about her, and why she is so great, and how I would try to be a great boyfriend if she would give me a chance. But it hurt so much when she called and broke our date last spring. No, I'm just not going through that again. For sure, Mia and Elly are the type of girls I would want to marry. Maybe I can find a girl like either one of them in college.

The second thing on my list is to have children and be a great dad. When my kids are little, I'll read to them every night before my wife and I put them to bed. Mom used to read to me before bedtime. I'll always remember those *Goodnight Moon* times. I'll help my wife with the kids' diapering and cleaning up the nursery and all those things so that my wife won't be overburdened. When my kids are older, I'll go watch them when they are in school plays or participating in sports.

I want to be a constant presence in their life, and for them to know that I will always be there for them.

Third, I want to be a teacher. There's probably about ten teachers at this school who would laugh their heads off at that goal, but that's what I want to be. I obviously haven't been the most dedicated student, but I've seen how good teachers teach and how bad teachers screw up. I can be a good teacher. Good teachers aren't sarcastic toward their students, and they respect them when they have ideas or opinions about something. They don't play favorites, and they're patient when a kid is having trouble with some difficult concept. I absolutely know I can be that type of teacher. I've struggled through a lot of my classes, and I know what kids need to succeed—encouragement and one-on-one help… being patient when some kid doesn't quite understand something the first or the fifth time.

Next, I want to live out in the country on a piece of land that has a creek flowing through woods. I want to be able to go out my back door and go fishing or hunting, or just sit out in the woods in the mornings and evenings to listen to birds singing and owls hooting. I want to have at least five or ten acres; 20 or 30 would be even better. I'd take my wife and kids walking through the woods, and we'd pick berries or look for edible mushrooms. Or we would go down to the creek and go fishing or seine minnows… maybe have water battles. I've always hated living in town, living in the 'burbs, even with Granddaddy. I just want to be in a place where I can roam around.

I'd like to share that life with a girl who is as special as Mia or Elly. But it's never going to be either one of them. Mia's probably going to end up being a doctor in Texas. And Elly will probably end up marrying some rich guy living in the suburbs. That's the kind of guy her dad would approve of, for sure.

I'm going to achieve my dreams. I'm not going to be poor forever. I'm not going to work some job I hate for 40 or 50 years, then keel over from a heart attack. I'm going to marry a great girl, have two or three kids, teach in a school, and live in my dream house out in the country. Nothing's going to stop me.

CHAPTER FIFTY-EIGHT

ELLY

On the last day of school, in English class, Paige, Kylee, and I sat over in a corner and talked the entire time. That is, as soon as Miss Roche gave up on trying to get us motivated to watch some movie. Over half the class was absent. Not many people ever come the last day of school.

Right when we started talking, I looked over and saw Luke. He had this intense expression on his face, and it was clear that he was thinking hard about something. I wish it were about me, but I know it's not. When I was looking at him, Paige said, "Why don't you go over and talk to him? We know you want to."

"I wasn't looking at Luke," I stammered.

"Oh, please. Give it up, girl," said Kylee.

"I don't know what you mean," I said.

"Elly, you've made so many stupid decisions about boys your whole time in high school," Paige said with this sarcastic tone in her voice. "Why don't you do something smart for a change and go talk to him? He's got it bad for you."

"He does not," I said.

"Really? That's not what Allen has told me," Paige said. "Those two guys have been best friends for years, and Allen has told me how Luke used to rave about you when all of us were freshman."

"That was a long time ago," I said. "We all were a lot different back then."

"Some things never change, though," said Kylee. "Some guys were sweet then, but we didn't realize it. Maybe it's because we wanted more flash in a guy. We'd get sucked in by their looks and their social status. We never saw the flaws those kinds of guys had. Those shy, really nice guys—they were like, you know, that phrase 'hiding in plain sight.' Luke's one of those guys. One day, you'll wake up and realize you've let him slip through your fingers."

"Like you let Marcus slip through your fingers," I said.

"That's a little harsh," said Paige.

"No, that's okay," said Kylee. "Yeah, obviously I was the one who broke up with Marcus this year. Maybe that was a mistake; maybe not. I just needed a change. For sure, it was a mistake to have dated him for so long when we were freshmen. But there was his charm, and sports-superstar status. His money. It was a big deal to go out with him in ninth grade. But he really was an insufferable jerk then.

"This year was different. I just needed to see what else was out there. He was really the only boy I've ever dated. Paige, Allen is the only boy you've ever dated. Come on, aren't there times when you wished you've dated other guys?"

I was shocked by what Paige said.

"Yes," she said. "Sometimes... well, many times, I do. I have these terrible doubts that one day, I'll look back and regret that Allen is the only boy I've ever dated. But other times, I think he really is a great guy. And he is. He has treated me really well. We really do care for each other. But, still... maybe. I don't know."

"Let's get back to the subject of you and Luke," said Kylee.

"I don't think we're through discussing you and Marcus," I shot back.

"Okay," said Kylee. "Do I sometimes regret breaking up with Marcus this year... yes. Am I sometimes jealous of him and Camila... yes. Do I sometimes dream of getting back together with him... yes. Am I sometimes glad that I decided to move on and see what else is out there... definitely yes.

"But my up-and-down relationship with Marcus can't be compared to you and Luke because you two were never official. All I'm saying is that no matter what happens with you and other guys in the future, there will always be these lingering doubts in your head that you let Luke get away. And if I were you, I wouldn't want to have that thought rattling around in my head a year or two from now."

"She's right," interrupted Paige. "Kylee's really, really right. I've seen how you two act together at games, in Yearbook. You two are the ultimate non-couple couple. Best-friends-forever type of couple. But you'll always regret that you didn't try to be more than friends if you don't make a move on him, Elly. I didn't think much of Luke when we were freshman. He's grown up now."

Then Kylee chimed in. "Look at all that has happened to him in high school. His father abusing him, his mom dying from cancer, his dad driving drunk and being killed in a car wreck. You told me that his grandfather has dementia. He's like 17 and basically living on his own and running a house. I bet he has to do all the grocery-shopping and bill-paying for his grandfather. None of us have had to live like that. It would have devastated me. Luke's still standing. He must have a fierce sense of self-survival."

"If he's so great, then why haven't you made a move on him?" I said. As soon as I said that, I realized that I was wrong. And I immediately apologized to Kylee.

"That's okay," said Kylee. "I realize you weren't thinking when you said that. But don't think I didn't think about making a move on Luke after I broke up with Marcus. Honestly, the reason I didn't is because I've seen how he looks at you, and how you two act when you're around each other. He's into you."

"She's right," said Paige. "Elly, you've got to go after him for your own sanity."

Paige is right. Kylee is right. I've got to make a move on Luke. And I definitely will, either this summer or next fall, when we get back to school.

CHAPTER FIFTY-NINE

MARCUS

Camila and I decided to blow off the last day of school on Wednesday and go to the state park and have fun. The school was basically empty for the past few days. The seniors graduated on Monday night; and obviously, they're not coming anymore. On Tuesday, we just sat around in all our classes and did busy work. Nobody, including the teachers, was into it. I told Mom that I was bored and going to skip Wednesday. She mumbled something about showing responsibility, but she knows that nothing's going on at school.

I've got a really busy summer coming up, and so does Camila. I just wanted to have a couple of days off before starting my summer jobs, sort of let my mind run free. But the weird thing was that Camila and I ended up doing all this heavy-duty talking and thinking about our futures. She's in choir, so she was at graduation on Monday night for all the pomp-and-circumstance stuff. She said speaker after speaker talked about the future of themselves and the class. The valedictorian even said that that night was the last one that all the members of the class would be together, but "such is life." Many of the graduates, the girl said, would be far, far away when the class's ten-year reunion came a decade from now. Statistically, the girl said, some of them would likely be deceased; but that, too, was part of life.

"That's pretty harsh stuff for a valedictorian speech," I said.

"But it's true, Marcus. Ten years is a long time. Where will you be ten years after graduation?" she asked.

It was a good question. When I was an obnoxious freshman, I would have said I would have been a 28-year-old wide receiver in the NFL. When not playing pro football, I would have been working on my announcing career for after I retired. God, how immature and unrealistic can one person be?

After a long pause, I said, "I could be working at a museum. I could be a history teacher at some college. Maybe I might be working on historical research somewhere. I could go into government work, maybe even working for the state department. I've got zero interest in teaching at a high school. I don't think I would have the patience to do that. How about you, Camila?"

"I'd like to be running my own business," she said. "Exactly what kind of business, I don't know. I know this is crazy; but I've also thought about being a lawyer, maybe helping out people who have been harmed by somebody who is corrupt or dishonest, or has faulty merchandise or something. I want to do something meaningful. What do you think about that, Marcus?"

"I think you'd be awesome as a lawyer. I sure wouldn't want to mess with you if you were wound up about something," I said, then laughed.

"That would be wise of you not to mess with me when I'm on a crusade," she said. Then she got real heavy with what she said next. "Can you see us being together ten years from now?"

I wasn't expecting that kind of deep question. She really caught me off-guard. Girls seem to think more about the future and relationships than guys do. It's true that they're more mature than we are. But I know I've grown up a lot in the last few years, too. I could tell that she was waiting for an answer, and nobody said anything for like a minute.

"I can see us being together all our senior year," I said. "I can see us dating during college, especially if you end up going to the university like I am. I can see us dating during college even if you don't go there. So, yes, I can see us being together ten years from now."

"Good, so can I," she said, and leaned over in the car and gave me a really big kiss on the cheek. "I think our relationship has real long-term potential. But I also know we're still really young, and that we still have to go through a lot of things. We still have to grow up. We're seventeen, and we have values and ideas about things. Who can say how we'll be a year from now, four years from now, 10 years from now? I'd like to think, like to hope, that we would continue to grow as people and continue to grow as a couple. I hope so. I'm sorry for being so deep today. It was just last night at graduation… it was a night for deep thoughts."

"I get it," I said. "I know, I know."

About that time, we pulled into the park. She said, "Enough of that; let's go have some fun. Let's go swimming first. I want you to see me in my new bikini."

You can bet I was down with that. Despite Mom trying to guilt me about skipping, I was pretty sure I had made the right decision to skip school before the new-bikini remark. Now I was definitely sure.

Camila and I had an absolutely awesome day. We went swimming for a couple of hours, in between lying on the beach and talking. She had made this great picnic lunch with some sort of Dominican chicken recipe as the high point. We bought snow cones at the concession stand, then hiked for a couple of hours along a trail. It was one of the best dates Camila and I've ever had.

CHAPTER SIXTY

MIA

My college classes ended two weeks before the high school classes did, and it was sort of surreal not to have to go to class until after lunch. I've been studying so hard for so long, and I've been so sleep deprived. Lately, I've been going to bed at around 8 and sleeping until 9 or 10 the next morning. I didn't realize how exhausted I was. Well, maybe I did realize it, but there was just no time for sleep.

Mateo has been asking me out every weekend since we went to prom. I've only been going out with him on either Friday or Saturday nights, but not both. Since things were sort of winding down a little bit at both schools, I've gotten in a couple of babysitting jobs in my neighborhood on weekends. I need to make some money before my two summer jobs start.

But another reason I've been babysitting is that I don't want to go out with Mateo so much, and need to have a ready excuse. I do like him. He is a good and kind person. He certainly is intelligent and he's very good-looking and has plans for the future. He wants to major in business and go into one of those fields where you help people manage their money. That's a high-paying job as everyone knows, and he would be really good at that sort of thing.

But here's the big *but*. Mateo doesn't make me thrilled to be around him. He says all the right things, does all the right things, but he doesn't wow me. Lately, he's been talking about the future and how great it is that we are both going to the same university. I know I have a full scholarship for college. I still need to be earning and saving money, but that knot in my stomach—that fear of never having enough money—won't be so bad anymore. I'll have four years to save money for graduate school. Because in graduate school, everybody will be really smart, and there will be a lot more competition for financial aid.

I could see myself still dating Mateo at the university. But would I be *settling* for him, sort of as the default guy? Honestly, with as hard and as long as I'm going to have to work to become a pediatrician, I probably will be one of those people who don't get married until she's 30. And when she's 37, she's worried that she hasn't had time to start having kids yet. I really want to be a mother. I've got a great mother, and I definitely could use her as a role model.

Sometimes, I think about the future. Then there are other times when I think of the things I want to happen in my senior year of high school. And that's when I think about Luke. We never had our follow-up conversation like we both said we wanted to have. Luke never says something unless he means it, so I am sure that he wanted us to talk some more.

I just feel like I won't ever be satisfied if I don't give him and me, us, another chance. The odds are astronomical that we would stay together all through my schooling. But if there was one boy I would make some accommodations for, it would be him. Elly says it looks like he's going to go to the local college. So Luke and I would only be a couple of hours' drive away from each other, and I know I'm coming home on some weekends. And he could come visit me.

The graduate-school years would probably be a real problem, though. That would be a real long-distance relationship. But if we built up and strengthened our relationship during our time in college; and if we found that we really, truly, and deeply loved each other, we could overcome the distance thing... couldn't we?

I absolutely know I could fall in love with Luke. I'm not sure I could ever fall in love with Mateo. I'm definitely going to talk with Luke some more... either over the summer or, if not then, when our senior year starts. I definitely don't want to regret never doing so.

Mama has said over and over how much she regrets marrying my father when she was so young. She had other boyfriends besides him at the time, and she liked one in particular a lot. That man, she said, is now a very successful businessman; and is still single, from what she hears. Who knows how different her life could have been if she hadn't made an impulsive decision when she was in high school?

Maybe I'll call Elly, Paige, Camila, Hannah, and Kylee and see if everybody wants to get together for an end-of-the-school-year sleepover. I could bring up the subject of Luke when we start dishing on boys—which will probably happen pretty early in the evening. Maybe I'll even call Luke tonight.

Or maybe I will just wait until next fall and my senior year to sort out all my feelings about Luke and everything else. I guess all of us will have to make some life changing decisions then about a lot of things.

S

CPSIA information can be obtained
at www.ICGtesting.com
Printed in the USA
FSHW011018270919

9 781944 962616